MYSTERY
OF THE

*B*ONE *S*CAVENGERS

Doris Holik Kelly

•A
Arbutus Press
Traverse City

BIG MITTEN MYSTERIES
BOOK # 3
Mystery of the Bone Scavengers © Arbutus Press 2010

Doris Holik Kelly
http://www.dorisholikkelly.com/

Cover illustration: Keith Jones
bigtimeartguy@bellsouth.net

ISBN 978-1-933926-26-1
Printed and bound in the United States

Arbutus Press
Traverse City, MI 49686

info@arbutuspress.com
www.arbutuspress.com

Also by Doris Holik Kelly
Big Mitten Mysteries

MYSTERY OF THE COPPER TURTLE

MYSTERY OF THE VOYAGEURS RENDEZVOUS

THE LOST IS FOUND AND LOST AGAIN

History term paper by Jared Daly.

L ife is all about bones. A skeleton of bones holds us together. Without our bones, we'd all be big lumps of goop laying on the ground, flopping about like weird fish.

The most valuable bones are those no one has been able to find—like all of Father Jacques Marquette's bones. When Father Marquette, the Guardian Angel of the Kiskakon Ottawa and the discoverer of the Mississippi River, died in 1675, his loving friends buried him on a sand dune overlooking Lake Michigan and marked the spot with a lonely wooden cross. Two years later, those Ottawa friends returned to the spot, gathered his bones, cleaned and washed them, and placed them in a birch bark box. When they returned to their home in Missilimackinak (St. Ignace), they buried the bones beneath the altar of the mission.

Two hundred years later in 1877, archaeologist Father Edward Jacker dug under the remnants of the burned mission into what he thought was Marquette's grave. Father Jacker and the workers found nothing but bits of birch bark and tiny fragments of bone.

Someone had stolen the remains of the Guardian Angel of the Ottawa.

Where did they go? Who took them, and why did they take them? Some people think the bones will never be found because they were buried deeper than normal or perhaps they were entirely destroyed by the fire that burned the mission chapel. Some have guessed they were taken by the local Ottawas who made relics of his bones, just as relics were made of the bones of the saints he taught them about.

Father Marquette had asked his friends not to forget him and they never did. His name graces a city, a bay, a university, high schools and elementary schools, hotels and banks, from Minneapolis at the beginning of the Mississippi River, to New Orleans, at the very end.

Why search for the bones of a man the world has never forgotten?

Maybe it's like hunting for, and finding buried treasure. It's the excitement of touching the past and making it a part of the present, or maybe it's just because they want to say they were the person who discovered the treasure.

CHAPTER ONE

I HATE RESEARCH!

"**R**esearch papers. Oral reports. Arrgh! I hate research!" I tossed my notebook down with a slam. "Can I report my teachers for mental cruelty?"

The guy across from me at the library table said, "Yo, Daly! Trying to study here! Can you dial it down a decibel?"

"Uh sorry, Hadsell.... It's been a rough day."

"Yeah, me too. I'm writing my biology paper on the decomposition rates of dead microorganisms. Do you want to trade?"

"Yuck. No thanks, Al. My brain is already decomposing. I'm supposed to write a ten page paper and all I've got so far is two pages!"

I pulled my chair up to the table in the library and buried my head in my hands. You'd think by tenth grade my brain would be so full of information I could just reach up into my head and pull out something brilliant. But no, I drew a blank. I gave up, packed my stuff, and headed for home.

When I got home from the library, I had an email from Eric Redhawk. *Yo, Fudge Breath. Aunt Dodo fell and broke her leg so now I'm here in St. Ignace helping her run Partridge's Bed and Breakfast Inn. You want to come help out, too?*

Yahoo! That's it! I could research Marquette and the mystery of his missing bones in St. Ignace. That's the kind of research I could really sink my teeth into— along with researching the local fudge, that is. I jumped up and down with excitement like my sister Sadie at a make-up sale.

"What's going on?" Sadie zoomed into my room as if she had been shot from a cannon. Her curly red hair stood on end as if it had exploded. She carried a lipstick in one hand and a bag of chips in the other.

"I'm going to St. Ignace!"

"Not without me, you aren't," she said.

"But I'm going for research."

"Sure you are. Researching the many kinds of fudge available in Mackinac." Sadie went to my mirror and put on orange lipstick.

"No, really. I'm going to research Father Marquette and what happened to his bones for my history research paper. And you and your jack-o-lantern lipstick can't go."

"Hmmpf! I'm telling Mom!" Sadie ran off screaming like a fuzzy Elmo doll whose talk button was stuck on screech.

CHAPTER TWO

KEEPING IT CLEAN

M e- Jared Un-cool Daly, who has never yet kissed a girl, got mononucleosis, the famous 'kissing disease' this spring. I had missed a lot of school and driver's training, too. I was too sick to work on my history paper so my mom had gone to school and got an extension on it for me. Since it won't be due until after we get home from St. Ignace, I would have plenty of time to help at the Inn and do research. I was going to pass my history class with flying colors.

Unfortunately, my mom had an email, too. We were all going to St. Ignace after school was out. Except my dad who would be doing his usual job of guarding the governor.

The day after I got Eric's email, Dad and I were heading out for some one-on-one basketball in the driveway. When we got outside, there was a big pile of garbage right in the middle of the yard. Just looking at the garbage gave me a headache.

Dad walked over to the pile and kicked it. "What a mess! Why doesn't anyone ever see these things happen?" Somebody had been playing dirty tricks on us recently. He put a cat in our garbage bin and when Mom opened it, the cat jumped out and scared her half to death. All our car door handles had been covered with syrup and grease was smeared all over Dad's windshield.

Then in the next second, the Michigan State Fight Song blasted out of his pocket. He yanked his phone out and acted as if he was going to fling it into the pile of garbage. He heaved a frustrated sigh and opened it. "Hey man, I'm off! What? Not again… Okay." The phone snapped shut and Dad glared at it. "I'm sorry, Jared, but I have to go into the office. Someone called in a threat at the capitol."

"But I thought that only happened during the day?"

"There is a big reception for a senator tonight. I put Carl Smith in charge, but the governor wants me there, too."

"I'm sorry. I'll miss beating you tonight."

"Yeah, me, too. Sorry I have to leave you and Sadie to clean this up by yourselves. Don't forget to put the garbage bin away when you're done. We have to stop the person responsible for these dirty tricks."

Clean it up now? Why can't I do it tomorrow?

He went into the house to tell my mom and left five minutes later, buttoning a clean shirt. As he drove away, Dad growled into his phone, "Do you realize I haven't had a whole day off for a month?"

Oh, well. It had to be cleaned up, so I got to it.

"Sadie? Sadie!" When I bellowed as loud as I could into the kitchen window, my throat started to hurt again. I still wasn't quite over the mono.

"What! I'm busy." She came around the corner carrying the newest bag of chips with her and crunching a mouthful.

"When you're done yakking with your BFF, Dad says you should come out and help me clean up the mess someone made in the front yard. Hurry up, I feel really rotten."

"What again? Okay. I'm talking to Becky Redhawk. She has more news from the island. Give me a half hour."

"A half hour? Aw, come on, I need your help now. Please?"

"Oh all right. I'll be there in a minute. Hey, Beck, Jared says 'Hi'."

In a minute? With Becky Redhawk? After we spent the summer with the Redhawk family on Mackinac Island a while back, and solved a major mystery together, we became very good friends. Now those two girls can yak for days about absolutely nothing.

Sadie and Becky are both 13 and totally opposite. That must be why they get along so well. Sadie has googly blue eyes and red hair, a quick temper and a wicked punch that comes out of nowhere. I know because I have been on the receiving end of that punch many times. Mom unleashed a monster when she gave Sadie permission to paint her face. She is crazy about makeup. Her lipstick and plastering trowel show up hourly.

Becky has dark brown eyes, wears her long black hair in braids and is a very natural looking person. I've seen her face get bright red when she's angry, but she never punches me. I'm thankful Becky doesn't have Sadie's makeup addiction. At least I can look at her without laughing. She never has lipstick on her teeth or raccoon eyes from mascara leftovers.

I scraped and shoveled the garbage until I was sick and tired of it. I decided to leave the rest for Sadie. When she strolled up with a gooey fluorescent pink lipstick smile on her face, I wanted to stick her face in the bathtub and scrub her makeup off.

"About time! Pierce a new hole in your ear?"

"Yeah, yeah, and a matching one in my nose."

I saw a quick vision of a red-haired cow in pink lipstick with an earring dangling from her nose. It was so funny I almost yelled, "MOO!" I couldn't help a snort and a grin and Sadie asked suspiciously, "What's so funny?"

"Never mind." I didn't want to start anything. Maybe later.

"Becky says there's a car show going on while we're up there."

"Cool. Will it be near us?"

"Yep, the whole town will be packed with all kinds of cars."

I looked around the yard. "Oh no… speaking of cars, take a look the dead squirrel on Mom's windshield."

"Ugh," Sadie shivered. "I'm not telling her about that mess. She'd never drive that car again."

"I cleaned all the other junk up, so that's your job!" I picked up the broom, shovel, and a bunch of old newspapers I'd been using to wrap up loose garbage and headed for the garage.

Sadie folded her arms. "No way! I'd need a hazmat suit! Flat dead squirrels are not in my job description."

"Aw, come on Sadie. I really don't feel well and I need to get busy on my research paper." I begged like a scared little kid. I knew if I touched that thing I'd barf.

She gave me a nasty grin. "No chance." She pointed at my chest with a blood-red polished fingertip. "But I will give you my mental support."

Funny. The chicken feathers in her brain couldn't hold up anything. I turned away and took a deep breath. My throat hurt more and more—I felt a relapse coming on. "All right….if I have to." *Sisters!*

Sadie pulled out a hand mirror and checked her face. "Come on, get on with it. I don't have all night. I have stuff to do."

The smell made me want to retch. I sighed and looked around. "All right, I'll do it." I grabbed a shovel and scraped it off the windshield onto some newspapers. I did it so fast I left skid marks in the paint.

"Take it easy, you're going to kill her paint job!"

"Hey, what are you kids doing? I'm going to tell your mother." The voice came from Miss Ruffle's yard.

Miss Adelaide Ruffle is our new weird neighbor. She and her brother Sky moved in a couple of months ago. I've never seen him because he's never home. I think she's bored because she's constantly peeking through the fence watching us. Dad says she looks like an 80's hair band guy named Dee Snider. She wears a gigantic curly blonde wig that is never on straight. It's like she sticks it on when someone comes to the door. She doesn't wear any makeup except bright red lipstick. But she should. Except for her enormous red nose, she looks just like a wrinkled Shar-pei dog. She wears baggy flowered dresses that almost drag on the ground, sometimes over a pair of pants. That's probably because she's hiding her wrinkled Shar-pei legs.

I ignored her. Mom says we have to be nice to Miss Ruffle because she's old and she can't walk very well. Mom gives her more homemade cookies than I get. After I mow Miss Ruffle's huge lawn she throws a fifty-cent tip at me and says, "Don't spend it all in one place!" Then she brays "Hee-haw! Hee-haw!" like a donkey and slams the door in my face.

Miss Ruffle screeched another angry outburst. "Don't ignore me, you bratty kids! You'll be sorry."

When I glanced at her all I saw was her wig, styled like an eagle's nest, and her beady eyes glaring at me. I had enough problems. I didn't need her razzing me.

I said, "We're not doing anything important." I dumped the wrapped dead squirrel into a garbage bag and threw up.

"Hee-haw! Hee-haw! Y'er one sick puppy, Mr. Know-it-all." I heard the jingle of her slippers and her back door slammed shut. She's not a nice lady.

Sick puppy? When Mom told Miss Ruffle I had mono, Miss Ruffle sent me a flower arrangement. I think she put poison ivy in the arrangement because I broke out in a rash. Sadie says Miss Ruffle gave me her cooties, not poison ivy. One of her windows is near my bedroom window and all I heard all day for two weeks were dying people screeching opera songs. I now hate opera. I was tempted to put that dead squirrel in Miss Ruffle's mailbox and see how she'd like it.

CHAPTER THREE

PARTRIDGE BED AND BREAKFAST

Driving north was a challenge. I spent hours cramped in the back seat of the car and still wasn't feeling all the great . At least with all the meds I swallowed, I wasn't contagious any more.

The night before we left for St. Ignace, Miss Ruffle gave us some cookies and I quickly deposited them in the garbage. I don't trust anything that weird woman makes.

I brought books on Marquette along on the trip but couldn't concentrate. I had cranked my I-pod as loud as I could without going deaf but I still kept hearing the wailing "ah-ah-ah-ah" of the operas in my brain. Mom drove like a maniac and sang along with her old Madonna and Whitney Houston CDs, and Sadie never stopped yakking and texting on her cell phone. I could not wait until we got to St. Ignace. I just wanted some place quiet to sleep.

As we drove across the beautiful five-mile long Mackinac Bridge it felt like I was home. At almost 200 feet above the cold blue lakes, I could see both Fort

Michilimackinac and Mackinac Island. They looked small and peaceful from that distance, but all through history neither one has ever been peaceful.

When we arrived on the north side of the bridge, we followed the long curving road that clings to the shores of Lake Huron and descends into downtown St. Ignace. Mom said that Father Marquette started his mission here in 1671, but this was major trading area for nomadic Native American tribes centuries before he arrived.

Our home away from home for the next few weeks, Partridge's Bed and Breakfast Inn, was on a small hill close to downtown St. Ignace. Mom went ahead to check us in while Sadie and I unloaded the car-top carrier. I piled as much luggage as I could on Sadie. Soon she looked like a little pack mule in full make-up.

Sadie carried my two suitcases and her makeup bag a couple of feet, but gave up. "I'm not carrying all this stuff. You carry your own things, Jared!" I'm sure her makeup bag weighed more than my suitcases together.

I carried a small bag of the things I can't live without, a notebook, and a stack of books. I didn't bring as much stuff as I did when the black garbage bags went to Mackinac Island our first time. This trip was supposed to be for two weeks and not the whole summer.

"But the doctor told me to rest."

Sadie sat down on the suitcases with a huge sigh "You could have stayed home and made me feel better."

"What, and miss all this?" I rubbed my hands gleefully together. "Not a chance. I love magnificent fudge. Besides, where is a better place to research Father Marquette? Some of him is buried here anyway. Very little, as I recall."

"Research? Ha! I still doubt you're up here for real research."

"Yes, I am. I'm going to research about what happened to all his bones."

She pointed at the big suitcases. "Get over here and carry these! They are too heavy for me."

"All right. But you'll have to carry everything else in."

She made a sour-pickle face at me with slimy pink lips and pointed at the house. "Not a chance! Move your bones, brother dork!"

"Okay, okay. I'm moving."

I hiked down the driveway to the porch of the bed and breakfast inn. I couldn't believe how that gigantic yellow house loomed above me. It was higher than Mount Everest.

"Wow, Sadie! I see now why their aunt needs help. This place is huge! Looks like you are going to be working hard while I rest."

"Suck it up, Jared. Everybody is going to work on this trip. Even you." Sadie practically skipped up the steps and sneered at me from the top.

CHAPTER FOUR

WELCOME HOME, FUDGE BREATH

As soon as the front door of Partridge's closed behind me, I yelled, "Hey, where is everybody?" I followed the wide hallway past the check-in desk to a huge living room lined with shelves full of books. I was in book heaven. There were also large woven baskets, blankets and all sorts of other Native American items scattered around the room like a mini museum. I saw a large drum in a corner, a small birch bark basket decorated with porcupine quills, an old cradleboard beaded with a flower design, and some feathered fans. I couldn't tell what was in the baskets.

I remembered how the last time we visited Mackinac Island someone stole Native American art pieces from the stores and Sadie, Becky, Eric, and I solved the mystery of the missing copper turtle. Sadly, many special things were never recovered.

When I made my grand entrance, Mom was over in the corner yakking with an older woman in a wheel chair. I deduced she might be informing on me when they looked my way.

"Whaa-hoo! It's Fudge Breath. Welcome home, dude." Eric leaped over some furniture and pounded me on the back. "Glad to see you've recovered. Who was the lucky woman who gave you the kissing disease?"

"Thanks, Pony Tail." I tossed the bag and the suitcases aside and shook his paw. Eric had hung up the black cowboy hat and lost the bad attitude, but he still had his long ponytail.

"Well, man, sorry to say, but I was dating so many beautiful women at the time, I never figured out who I got it from."

"Whoo-hoo, dork! Mom's going to wash your mouth out with soap!" Sadie yelled from the tattletale corner.

Eric snorted, "Heh, heh. Gotcha, old man. Our sisters are going to squeal on you. Uhh, Jared?" He pulled me aside. I thought he had something serious to discuss.

"Huh?"

"While you're here, make sure you kiss my sister. She's been irritating me way too much." I must have turned red because Eric laughed like a lunatic, slapped me on the back, and ducked out of my reach.

"Fun-ny, Pony Tail." Great. Eric hadn't changed a bit.

Becky ran up and gave me a hug. "**Boozhoo!** Welcome, Jared. Sorry about the mono. I've missed you and Sadie. Aunt Dodo put you and Eric on the first floor so you can staff the desk for her in the afternoon when

20

she naps. Your mom is on the second floor and Sadie and I are upstairs in an attic dorm room."

"Thanks, Becky, I missed you, too." I could feel my freckled face getting hotter by the second and my glasses started steaming up. I had forgotten how cute she was. "I appreciate the lower floor. I'm still kind of tired."

"We'll take good care of you, Fudge Breath," Eric said. "Maybe you can help us figure out what's going on down the hill in Dr. Teya Dove's new dig. The infamous Dr. D. just showed up one day, announced that she's Cousin Luke's fiancée, and said he gave her permission to dig in Aunt Lulu's yard for fun. She says it's a private dig and won't let anyone else near it."

"Is that legal?"

Becky scowled. "Maybe legal, but probably not right. Aunt Lulu's land is next to Marquette Park. We think her land used to be part of the old mission grounds. But it doesn't matter where anyone digs; every part of this town is ancient and they always dig up something."

"Yeah," Eric said, "we think the strange woman is planning to dig up some real trouble."

CHAPTER FIVE

EERIE PEOPLE

I went into my room, threw my suitcases on the bed and went over to my window. What a view. A block to the east, I saw several old homes, an arrangement of tents near one of them, the old Museum of Ojibwa Culture building, and Father Marquette Park next to it. At my right was a hardware store and parking lot. Across the street to the left were the Little Bear Hockey Arena and a small grove of trees. Beyond that, I saw Lake Huron, the Indian Village Store, the harbor, ferryboats, and all the way to Fudge Island—uh, Mackinac Island.

"Ahh, if only I could reach across the water and into a fudge shop, my life would be complete right now."

Eric went back home to the island for the night and I thought I'd take a short hike down to visit the dig before I started working at the Inn.

The odd-looking campsite was drawing me in. One small tent was near a house and two other large tents were next to the property line, so close they were almost sitting in Marquette Park.

A tall thin man wearing dark glasses and black hooded sweatshirt came out of one of the large tents followed by a short female in a dark glasses, wide straw hat and long sleeved work clothes. I could tell she was yelling at him even though I couldn't hear the words. One minute she jabbed her finger at him as if she was pecking a hole in the air and the next her arms flapped around as if she were planning to be airborne. It reminded me of the chicken dance we do at weddings. The skinny man looked at her and laughed. He picked up something off a folding table and went into the other big tent. The girl stomped down the street and went into a building.

Hmm. I wonder what they could be looking for? Everything I've read says there have been ten digs in thirty years on that site. What could be left to find? Guess I'll go see. No sooner had I stepped down the front steps than I heard a voice from above—and it wasn't an angel.

"Hey, Jared, where are you going?" Sadie yelled out from the attic window.

"Down there! I want to see what's in the tents!"

Becky poked her head out next to Sadie. "Alone?" she asked. "You're going to the site alone? No way! Teya gave me strict orders to keep you away from her dig."

"Too bad! I'm sorry she has such a rotten attitude. But that is a public street and that's a public park."

"Wait, Jared, I want to go, too," Sadie screeched.

"No! You stay here. I want some peace and quiet for a while."

I hurried down the sidewalk as fast as I could, but the girls charged out the front door and caught me.

Becky stepped in front of me, "Jared, you don't understand. You won't get any peace and quiet down there. Teya's evil, nasty, and she hates white people."

I couldn't believe what I was hearing. "So she's prejudiced?"

Becky sighed and shifted around as if her shoes were too tight. She looked at the ground and mumbled, "Yes and no... I thought it was because she was new to town and shy. But since then I figured out that she's just plain horrid."

"But nasty only to whites, not natives?"

Becky reluctantly nodded. "Uh... yeah... so far. Guess you could say that." She looked embarrassed.

"If she believes her race is better than anyone else's that's called racial prejudice. Now if I did it, I'd be in major trouble because that's not allowed anymore. Do you remember what you told us when we first met? That we weren't allowed to be rude and tease about 'Indians.'"

"I know it's wrong for her to feel that way, but I'm warning you—she's awful!" Becky punched me gently on the arm.

"So Jared Daly, who is descended from the Irish, Polish, and all kinds of other nationalities, shouldn't go down there?"

"Well. She doesn't know you yet. You understand, don't you, Fudge Breath?"

"Come on, back off, Jared," Sadie said. "She must have her reasons."

"Sure, she has reasons—she's prejudiced…. Okay. I'll be good." *If I have to.*

"Whew!" Becky looked relieved. "I'm telling you guys, I don't like or trust her. Teya has strange jumpy eyes. I get a creepy slithery feeling in my stomach when she stares at me. So don't antagonize her. She'll probably attack and bite you or something."

I looked at Becky a long time while she looked awkwardly anywhere but in my face.

"Okay, I give up…. But I think there's more to this story than you're telling us." I stuck out both elbows. "Will you strong women escort and protect me from the evil Dr. Dove?"

Sadie said, "Careful, Jared, or we'll think you're planning something."

"I think you should not stress your tiny brain, Sadie." Whack! She swatted me on the shoulder. "Ouch, cut it out!"

When we got to the site, the spookiest woman I had ever seen met us.

"Get out of here! Don't make me hurt you!" Teya stalked up to us, grabbed Becky's arm and pulled her away from us. "You! You nasty white people! Stop touching her and get away from my dig!"

CHAPTER SIX

WATCHING THE WENDIGOS OR ARE THEY VAMPIRES?

I looked at her and laughed, "Who is calling who nasty?" I asked.

Such a strange-looking woman with all her layers of black clothes. She shot an evil look at me. Her black eyes were half hidden behind thick glasses, but I still felt her anger.

Becky yanked her arm away and straightened up. "Stop it, Teya. I know you're being careful, but you have to settle down. No one has touched anything."

Teya put her nose in the air and spat out, "But I am Luke La Croix's fiancée and this is his home. They are trespassing!"

I couldn't believe she was real. "Big whoop. Luke is nothing special."

She stared daggers at me and inhaled loudly through clenched teeth. It sounded like a hiss.

Becky said, "Settle down, Teya. We're leaving. Sorry, guys. Let's go. She'll get over it."

As the girls and I hiked back up the hill, we could hear Teya start arguing with the skinny guy who had returned.

"Jared, did you know I stuck my tongue out at her?" Sadie said with a giggle.

"No. Did it make you feel better?" When she laughed, I said, "Go ahead and do it again for me."

I grabbed my Marquette Mission Site information and got busy at the living room desk when we got back to the house. I didn't have a lot of time to finish the paper and it was 75 percent of my grade.

Teya's site couldn't be a real site since all the ground in this area is sacred to the Ottawa and Ojibwa population. St Ignace had been a spring rendezvous place for northern tribes like the Huron, Potawatomi, Sac and Fox, and more western tribes like the Lakota and Sioux for thousands of years. Everything I read said it was wrong for anyone to dig a shovel into the valuable ground without permission from the city, state, and the local elders of the community.

Later that afternoon I heard a 'ding-ding' from the bell at the front desk and heard Aunt Dodo and Becky check someone in who sneezed a lot.

"…no cats! I can't stand cats! Allergic to cats. Keep 'em away from my room! Hachoo!"

"Yes, sir!" I heard Becky say. "Yes, sir, we'll take care of it, sir."

"Becky, put this gentleman in room four off the dining room."

I agree with him. No cats!

"I prefer, ahh, ahh ….tranquil…room, Mesdames," another voice said.

"Yes, sir. Will the last room in the back of the inn be all right? You have a private entrance and it's very quiet back there."

"Parfait!" the man answered.

A few minutes later Becky strolled into the living room to talk while I had the Partridge's telescope focused on the dig site. "What'cha looking at?"

"Not much. I don't understand what's going on. It's a warm sunny day and they aren't digging or doing anything. Eric said they get up after three in the afternoon, go into the tents, and never come out until the sun is setting. Are they hiding something?"

"I don't know, but it sure makes me think they're doing something they don't want anyone to see. Teya's brother is the tall boney guy. His name is Thomas but he's nicknamed Dude. He's really scary. I'd swear he's a Wendigo or a vampire."

I put the glasses down, looked at her and snorted. "Come on… Wendigo or vampire? They look sort of Goth…, but vampires? I don't think so."

"Don't tease me, Jared! I don't like it." The flush of red that came over Becky's face reminded me of our first meeting.

"Calm down, Becky. I didn't mean to make you angry. What's the matter?"

"They don't make sense. Teya is so thin you can almost see through her. She is always dressed in black with long sleeves and long pants no matter what the temperature. Her face is tan and doesn't look vampire pale but her hands do. Dude never comes out of his tent on a sunny day. He's completely bald and very pale skinned, wears really thick dark glasses, and his eyes look odd… as if he's wearing white contact lenses. He's always drinking something red and slimy from a bottle. He says, "Mmm, I love my vitamins," and when he smiles, his teeth look bloody like the Gibi's did back on Mackinac Island. I never see him eat anything but jerky and pork rinds."

"Pork rinds?"

"Yeah, that nasty stuff. He says he likes to eat meat and *flesh*, like Hannibal Lecter in that gross cannibal movie. When I'm around him he always makes that strange sucking sound and laughs low and spooky. He gives me some major creeps."

"Okay. That creeps me out, too. Explain Wendigo. That's a new one to me."

"Ah-choo!" The sneeze was very loud. Mr. Sneezy Man must have been close by, but when we looked at the doorway, he wasn't there. Becky was very solemn and she spoke quietly, "A Wendigo is a cannibal that looks like a walking skeleton. He doesn't have any lips 'cause he ate them off. Tribal stories say he walks around during the long cold winter looking for starving people to turn into Wendigos like him."

I put my face in my hands and peeked at her through my fingers to keep her from seeing my smile. "Well…heh-heh, since your aunt planned all the meals, my mom's cooking, and this is June, I think we'll be okay."

I could feel Becky get angry. When her eyes got big and started to bulge, and her face turned a slight purple, I yelled, "Darn it, Becky, you Ojibwas have a lot of cannibals running around up here!"

I remembered the green Gibi who trapped us in the Haunted Hall on Mackinac Island and it still creeped me out. He was a cannibal, too. I had read old stories about Gibis who liked to cook people in a big pot at the Devil's Kitchen on Mackinac Island.

Becky slapped the table next to me and shouted, "Jared! Will you stop and think about it?" Then her voice got very soft and I could barely hear her. She said, "What if he really is something like that?" She stared beyond me and her eyes grew bigger as if she saw something outside the window and it was gazing back at her.

I felt almost hypnotized when I looked into her dark eyes. A shiver ran down my spine. Was Becky going crazy?

I had to stay calm. My imagination always ran ahead of me. She had me picturing Dude as a pale thirsty vampire biding his time waiting for a nice warm bloody meal. Or was he a hungry cannibal, planning to chomp on a human leg like it was a big turkey leg? Ugh. I could even see him lurking on the porch and watching me through my window while I slept.

Were we were going to be his next victims?

CHAPTER SEVEN

THE HURONS AND THE HEEBEEJEEBEES

"S-stop it, Beck, you're freaking me out!" My voice broke and I squeaked, "Duh- do you go down to the dig site very often?"

Becky sighed and collapsed onto a chair. The normal Becky was back. She wrinkled up her nose as if she was downwind of a smelly skunk.

"No way! Not if I can help it. I'll go with Eric or someone bigger like you, but not alone. Eee- yuck!"

Is a bigger person less appetizing to vampires? I hope so.

"Did you tell my sister anything about Dude?" I wanted to tell her about the Wendigo just to see her grossed out.

"Yeah. She thinks it's funny, too. But I went to a sleepover last winter and saw that sick-o Hannibal cannibal movie and she's never seen it. Will you watch the site and those weirdos for me, Jared?"

I had to smile at her. "I guess so." I can't refuse that shiny clean face. But the idea of vampire-watching gave me goose bumps the size of marbles.

"Well, I'm going to my Anishinabe language class, so **Gigawabamin Nagutch**. That means, 'I'll see you later,' Fudge Breath." Becky left, leaving the door open.

"Whew!" I took a deep breath. Becky is learning a lot about her family's heritage. And a lot of other strange stuff, too.

I took the telescope to my room and focused downhill again to see what was going on by the tents. I almost fell off my chair when a fluffy gray cat leaped onto my shoulder and rubbed his face on me. I shoved him off as fast as I could. I knew I had about 30 seconds before I lost control of my face. I grabbed a hanky and held on to my nose. Ahh-choo, ahh-choo. "Help somebody! Get this cat out of here! Ahh-chooo!"

When I yelled and sneezed, the cat ran to the corner of my room and I headed for my stash of allergy meds.

"Please! No cats!" I howled out the door. Maybe the tuna I had for lunch brought him in to me.

Aunt Dodo rolled her wheelchair into my room and the furry feline jumped into her lap and nibbled on her fingers. "Sorry. Huron is supposed to stay outside. We have a new guest who just checked in and he's allergic to cats, too. I'll try to keep him away from you as well."

"Hur-hachoo! Sorry, can't stop sneezing. You call the cat Huron. Isn't that your tribe's name?"

"No. We are a mix of Ottawa and Ojibwa families here in the straits. The Wyandot or Huron Indians escaped from the Iroquois and came here with Pere

Marquette. They moved with Cadillac to Detroit about 30 years later.

"The word Ouendat or Wyandot meant 'unknown language' because no one understood them. But the French voyageurs jokingly called them 'Hure', or funny head. It referred to the way the Wyandot men wore their hair, rough and spiked up like a boar's hair. It looked foolish or funny to them," Aunt Dodo said.

"Which means that Lake Huron is Lake Funny Head. Whoo-hachoo! That really is funny!" I had to laugh and sneeze at the same time.

"Yes, it is funny. See, Huron has curved back ears and spiky ear hair. He's an American Curl cat. Now, you watch out for him. He's very mischievous and friendly. If he loves you, he'll never leave you alone."

"Speaking of Father Marquette, I'm doing a paper on his missing bones. I heard that when he died, someone dug up his bones and moved them."

"Yes, he died on his way back to Michilimackinac from Illinois in 1673. He was buried on the Lake Michigan shore near a small river. Some people say he was buried in Ludington, some in Frankfort, but another person who has researched more than anyone else says Marquette was buried in Manistee. The Kiskakon Ottawa knew where he was buried and they dug him up in 1675, washed his bones and brought them back to what is now St. Ignace. They put his bones in a birch bark box and buried the box beneath the altar of his chapel which sat by the water where the park is now.

"Twenty-eight years later, an angry priest burned down the chapel. Some people think most of Marquette's bones burned up in the fire. Two hundred years after Marquette's death when Father Jacker, an archaeologist, dug up the site, he only found tiny pieces of bone. Later, a man brought him some more small pieces of bones that he had found. Some of those little bones are now at Marquette University and some are still here, but they never found anything bigger than fragments. It's like the bones disappeared."

"Doesn't anyone have any other clues as to what happened after the fire?"

"Both museums here in town have information and I have lots of books out in the living room. Help yourself." She tightened her grip on Huron and wheeled out of the room.

Later, after my allergy meds kicked in, I looked downhill again. Dude stood in the tent opening out of the direct sunlight. He was so pale and thin his face almost disappeared into the white fabric of the tent.

I had to agree with Becky. "He looks just like a vampire… or something."

Chapter Eight

Gargoyles and zombies

The next day after I did all the dishes from breakfast and cleaned up the dining room, I began reading a book on Ireland. I needed to take a break from all my thinking about Marquette. How did I ever think I could solve a 200-year-old history mystery?

I wondered why Becky was involved in her family's history and culture and Eric could care less. Eric should have a little interest in it. I liked Irish history and I'd even like to go there someday. I might even kiss the Blarney Stone because it's supposed to give you the eternal gift of gab. I wondered if it would help me talk Sadie into giving up her makeup. Ha!

I must have dozed off, because I jumped when I heard Dude shout, "Hey, Aunt Dodo, You got any indoor work I can do? I'm running out of cash and my sister won't bankroll me any more this week."

"Sure come on in, Thomas. We can talk it over. I took a pie out of the oven. Want some?"

"Yeah, I dig pie."

"I have a lot of painting to do around here. Can you paint?

"Yep, I can paint…"

"Good, let me fetch the pie for you first."

All the rest of the morning while Dude painted, Aunt Dodo kept asking, "Would you like a fan? Do you need any more paint, Thomas? I took a cake out… got some cookies…you want a pop?"

Why would Dude want to eat a human being when he was already stuffed with goodies? Seems like a big waste of time to me. First, you'd have to chase a person down and then find a big pot…and then…it might get really gory.

Never mind. It seemed like lot of hard work to me.

I went out to the stairway and looked up to the third floor. Dude was on scaffolding up near the ceiling.

It made me dizzy to look at him up there. All I could think to say was, "Hey, Dude. Be careful man. Don't want you to fall."

Dude looked down, shuddered a little and said, "Yeah, it is a long way down there, but I'm not scared of heights." He squeezed his eyes half shut, wrinkled his pointy nose and with a slightly evil grin said, "I'm pretending I'm a bat clinging to this wall. You like vampire bats, Jared?"

Ugh, there go those marble-sized goose bumps. I took a deep breath, then said, "They're all right, if they stay outside where they belong."

I tried to ignore Dude's question and the fact that he somehow looked like an actual bat …or an evil-looking gargoyle as he perched up on that scaffold. His skeleton-like white fingers clutched the paintbrush and dipped it into what Aunt Dodo called Cranberry Soufflé paint. It looked like pinkish blood stroked onto the walls. It would not be my choice to paint an upstairs hallway. I'm more of a fan of blue water and blue skies …not bloody red.

After Dude had been working for about an hour I heard someone come in. I walked into the hallway and politely said, "Hello. Welcome to Partridge's Bed and Breakfast Inn." It was Teya rushing in the front door.

"May I help you?"

Her waist length black hair swayed across her back as she turned and gave me a fierce look. It might have curled my hair if it didn't already look like a bush.

"Get away from me, ugly fat man!" She yanked off her thick dark glasses and yelled, "Dude! Bro! Come down for a minute. I have news!"

It was almost 90 degrees outside and she wore a wide brimmed black hat, black long sleeved sweater, and gloves as if it was about 30 degrees.

I stood there and waited patiently. I figured if I stayed calm she would be nicer. She looked at me with a curled lip, "Never mind, Dude. I'm coming up. Too many big ears down here."

I was so amazed at her rudeness I think my mouth fell open. Why would she insult me? But if that was how she wanted to play it—I can give back as much as I get.

A couple of minutes later Dude jogged down the stairs shouting, "Yahoo! I gotta real job!" He ran out the door without a word to Aunt Dodo about leaving. Teya strolled grandly down the stairs with her head held high like a queen. She stared at me again and snarled, "What are you looking at, o' great rotund one?"

I said, "I'm not quite sure…. You are definitely not queen of the fairies because you don't have wings, so I think you are the queen of the zombies. But again, no body parts are falling off, so I have no idea who or what you are." I walked back into my room and shut the door.

I had to laugh when I heard a loud, "Brains!" as she left the building.

Well, she has a sense of humor. Maybe she's not dangerous after all. On the other hand, maybe she wasn't hungry right then.

Dude didn't come back to finish the job. But he did leave bloody dripping red letters on the white wall that spelled out, "Dude was here and now he's gone!"

Chapter Nine

What is a Medicine bag ?

That afternoon, when we were done cleaning the house, Becky yelled down the big curved stairs in Partridge's B&B. "Hey Jared, come up here! I want to show you something!"

She was two flights up but it sounded as if she was next door.

"Do you have an elevator?"

"Nah! Hop on up, Jared. We'll wait."

Climbing stairs made me very tired so I took my time.

Something crunched and I picked up a brown chunk similar to crispy dog food. Another pork rind. I stuck it in my pocket until I could throw it away.

When I got to the attic dormitory room, Sadie was drooling over the necklace Becky was wearing. "Oh, that is such a cool necklace. Where did it come from?" Sadie touched the three-strand necklace.

"Mom let me borrow the Redhawk wedding necklace to show you." Becky lifted the long strands of red, white, black, and silver beads. "We just had it re-strung by Beavo's Fine Jewelry. The Redhawk family brides have passed it down for about 250 years. I'll wear it someday, too. Mom lends it out to family brides. She's the boss in our family anyway." She grinned up at me as if she expected me to comment about women being in charge.

I held up my hand. "I'm not stepping in that one, Beck." But it *was* hard to keep a straight face.

"If Teya and Luke get married, she can wear it only during the ceremony. But I sure hope they don't get married."

"Does Teya know about the necklace?" I was curious.

"I don't know. Maybe Luke told her, but I don't trust her. Luke will have to come home and tell us that she's his fiancée first. Aunt Lulu said Teya brought a letter from Luke, but he hasn't answered his phone in weeks so she has no idea if Teya is lying or not."

"Is it unusual for Luke to not answer his phone? He could call back later."

"It's not unusual. But it has been longer than normal."

Sadie touched the bird pendant that dangled between the two largest gleaming red beads. "What is this red hawk made of?"

"It's Catlinite, sometimes called pipestone because a lot of tribes made their peace pipes from it. It came here from Minnesota through the trade route. In the Ojibwa language, it's called **Opwagunahsin**. The rest of the necklace is made of red jasper, bone, trade beads and silver."

Becky looked nice in the wedding necklace, but I wasn't going to tell her. My red face probably said it all.

"Yep," I said smiling at her. "What's the other necklace you're wearing?"

"Oh this?" She pulled a small tan bag on a leather string out of her shirt. It had a small red bird design beaded on the front. "It's my medicine bag."

"Medicine bag? Do you keep your medicine in there? It's kind of small."

"Well, sort of…I can't tell you what's in mine, but I can tell you what kind of special items people put in their bags."

Sadie laughed and said, "Mom's would be headache pills, toothpaste, arthritis cream, bug spray, paint, a brush and canvas…."

"Yeah. But this is more like the old medicines. A special rock, like a moonstone or a crystal, shells, feathers, leaves from the four sacred plants. Some people put a bone or a piece of someone's hair from a family member in their bags."

"Bones? Yuck!" Sadie made a face.

"They did that a long time ago."

"That is spooky! Hope you don't have any in yours."

"I couldn't tell you if I did. It's private." Becky grinned, "Remember, it is always items special to the owner."

"In dorky-bro Jared's case, he'd have a chunk of fudge… a quart of ice cream…and a book on baseball," Sadie went on.

40

"Stop it, Sadie. You're going to offend Becky."

"Gee, Jared, don't get so excited, "Sadie said. "Becky might think you like her."

"Ah-hem, ignore her, Beck." My throat needed clearing. "What happens in a Native American wedding ceremony? What makes it so special?" I had to sidetrack the women, it was getting too deep in there.

"Oh, promises, like a regular wedding. Do you remember how Aunt Dodo walked through the house and smudged it with **Mushkodaywushk,** sage, **Ahsayma,** tobacco, **Gisheekandug,** cedar, and **Weskwu mashkoseh,** sweet grass this morning? It was to purify the house and chase away the bad spirits. They do the same thing during a wedding. A special white wedding blanket is wrapped around the couple to show how they will share their lives. Songs are played on a cedar wood flute. It's usually different for each couple."

"How do you know the right words for those things?" Sadie asked.

"I learned those words in my Anishinabe (first nation) Ojibwa language classes. I go every other day in the summer down at the museum and we have classes during the school year, too."

"Will you teach us some words?" I thought it would be interesting to learn a new language.

Becky grinned. "Sure, if you want to. **Migwetch** means thank you."

"**Migwetch**, and you're welcome," Sadie said.

"It's time to get downstairs," Becky said. "I'll put the necklace right here in the bottom drawer of my nightstand under my stack of comics. You are the only ones who know where it is so it should be safe."

"Ouch!" a voice yelled outside the door.

We all turned to look and whoever it was thudded down the steps in a hurry.

Becky slammed the drawer shut. "Hey! Who's out there?"

Before we could open the door, we heard the downstairs screen door slam shut.

Charging out the door, we hurried to the staircase.

"Mee-ee-yow-yow! Mee-ee-yow-yow!" A big white fluffy cat twisted between my legs and almost tripped me.

"Oh no! Not another cat! You didn't tell me there would be cats at the Inn!"

"Oh sorry, Jared. We didn't know you're allergic to cats," Becky said. "Get down, Naggy!"

I grabbed my handkerchief and honked my nose, "Naggy? Does she complain a lot?"

"No, it's for **Nagamoon,** the Ojibwa word for song. She sounds like she's singing when she meows."

Naggy picked something up off the floor and sat down to eat it.

"What's that you have there, Naggy?" Becky leaned down and pulled something from the cat's mouth. "It's brown and looks like meat or something."

"Ha choo!" I rubbed my nose on my sleeve. "You mean like this?" I held out the piece of pork rind from my pocket. "I found this on the floor on the way up here. Somebody must have dropped it…"

Becky yelled down the staircase, "Hey Aunt Dodo, did you see who went down the steps and out the door?"

"What? I'm in the kitchen!" her voice was muffled from so far away.

Huron came out of a room near us, touched his nose to Nagamoon's nose, and glided down the stairs in a hurry as if he was chasing something.

"Hey, Huron, where are you going?" I knew he couldn't answer me, but he did.

"Meowt," he said as he looked up at me from the bottom step, pushed the screen door open and left.

"Did he say 'me out'? I never knew cats could talk."

"Of course they do, goofy." Sadie smacked my shoulder.

"Aunt Dodo is no help, but Huron's hunting for the suspect," Sadie said. "It sounded like the guy was in a hurry the way he thumped down the steps. Nobody's staying up here but us girls, right Becky?"

"Yeah. But we only have half of the attic. When the car show starts, the other room will be packed with people. It has ten beds in it, and only one bathroom."

Sadie made a face. "Eew. No privacy."

"Yeah, but most car show guys don't care. They only want a place to crash. Sleep, that is."

I went to the window that looked over the street. "There are a couple of people wandering around out there. A man in a white van is pointing at the tents and yelling at Dude. Ouch! He got out, slapped Dude, and left in a hurry. "

Becky peeked under my arm. "It looked like someone driving a city utilities truck but there's no sign on it. What are they up to now?"

"I'm going to go see. Bye!" And I left so they couldn't think of anything else for me to do.

CHAPTER TEN

CRAZY CAR SHOW

I followed Huron down to the dig site to do a little nosing around. Dude was sitting in a folding chair holding an ice bag to his pasty-colored cheek.

"Hey Dude. What happened?"

"Eh... Mr. Jacques...mm- Fountaine, who says he's from the city, delivered his own personal message right to my face. He, uh...says we're digging in the wrong place..., afraid we'll hit a gas or water line."

"Yeah. I guess that's possible, but you are pretty far off the road."

I looked up at the back door and saw Teya inside staring back at me. I waved and smiled and she turned her back to me. I got the message.

"Hey, Dude, I might as well ask this now as later. What exactly is Teya looking for?"

"You know, Jared, I've been asking the same question since we arrived and all I get is, 'I'll know it when I find it.' And what IT is, I have no idea."

"Well, from what I can see, she's looking for a grave, because as close as you are to the mission, there has to be an ancient cemetery nearby."

"Yep. I thought of that, too. So I'm watching..." I heard him mumble, "And digging like a mole..." as he got up and went toward the house rubbing his bruised face.

"When he opened the door, Teya yelled at me, "Go away, el lardo!"

"What a child."

Dude sighed and said, "I agree even though she's five years older than I am. It's too bad she's always so angry about everything." and he went inside.

Well, that told me nothing.

I went back up to the Inn and holed up in my room. Sometimes I still felt as if someone had run me over with a truck. I must have dozed off again while reading, but the loud sounds of engines revving, screaming car brakes and pounding music woke me straight up. I usually only heard the horn from the ferry coming and going, and nothing else. I went over to the window. In the distance, I saw a whole line of shiny cars drive past.

I changed my shirt and hurried to the dining room where lunch covered the buffet. Mom, Sadie, and Becky were doing most of the cooking as Aunt Dodo supervised. My job always came afterward—cleaning up the table and dishes. Ton's of them. I don't know why I ever agreed to this job.

"Hey, Pony Tail, what gives with all the cars out front? Has the car show started already?"

Eric took a bite of a bacon burger and chewed with his eyes closed. "Your sister makes a great burger. Yep, it starts tomorrow," he mumbled. "This one is for antique and muscle cars from the 50's and 60's. Dad has a blue '68 Chevrolet Camaro stashed in Aunt Dodo's garage. It has a big 396 engine. He shows it every couple of years, but he's too busy with some new things at home to mess with it this year."

"So what's planned for this show?"

"The usual. Hundreds of people and a gazillion cars parked everywhere on the streets and in the parking lots. Bands. A long parade cruise over the bridge to Mackinaw City. A deejay with loud ancient music and dance contests. Prizes for top car. Some people sell their cars here. Lots of smelly gas fumes, exhaust and noise. It all gives me a headache. I'd rather smell horse manure."

"I guess you would. But at least you got your driver's license and can drive that fancy car sometime. I'm bummed that I couldn't take my classes."

"Yeah, that's too bad. Don't plan to use my license with a car. Only need it to drive a buggy."

"Right... but what if you want to leave the island and come visit me someday? How do you plan to get there?"

"Bus."

"Hmm. Okay, that makes sense."

I'd stuffed half a banana in my mouth when the loud 'lub-dub-dub' rumble of a big engine and sound of squealing tires ripped through the room. Eric and I went to the windows that overlooked the street.

In the La Croix's driveway an old red Cadillac hearse with brilliant gold lettering on the side sat shining like a piece of warm cherry pie.

"*The Boney Collector*? Nice car. Great lettering. I wonder who's driving that slick machine." All the windows were blackened and mysterious. I was completely confused until the driver's door opened and Dude jumped out dressed in a hooded red satin jumpsuit and a black cape. The suit was so tight I could almost see every bone in his body because there sure wasn't any muscle on the poor guy.

"Look at Dude's car!"

Eric snorted, "What a wiener," and stalked back to the table.

Yep, he looked like one... in a batman cape.

I watched Dude stride up to the big tent and go inside. He came out a minute later, backed the car up to the tent and opened the hatch. I couldn't see what went in or out of it because I was at the wrong angle and way too far away.

CHAPTER ELEVEN

INVADE THE DIG

I never knew a house could be so full of people. I was at the check-in desk most of the day. The dorm room next to Becky and Sadie had six men in it and the fifteen other rooms were full, too. We tripped over car people in every room of the house. They were all there to have fun.

I was tired, but the book I was reading was interesting and there was enough noise in the house to keep me awake until midnight.

Someone whispered, *"Becky! Becky, where are you?"* outside my window. I was reading a hokey old book from 1937 called *Blackrobe*. It was about Father Marquette and pretty awful fiction. The book was disrespectful and so embarrassing to the Indians, I didn't want Becky or Eric to read it. I guess I should have shut my window, but instead I decided to scare the whisperer.

I stuck my face against the screen and roared, "Whaa!"

"Eeek!" Sadie squeaked like a scared mouse. Then she smacked the screen right by my nose. "Be quiet, Jared," she whispered.

Eric shot straight in the air, "Whaa? You woke me up! Would you be quiet? I have to work tomorrow!"

"Sorry, Eric. Ouch! Sadie, dat's my node." I felt my nose carefully. It seemed to be a little bruised but still in one piece. "What's up?" I decided to whisper, too, so I could keep my nose. "Why are you outside? The mosquitoes are killers out there!"

Becky snuck up and hissed right by my ear! "Shush, **Chinodin**, you big wind bag." And then she giggled like a monkey. "Eep- eep- eep!"

"New word, Beck?"

"Yeah, I don't think the tribe has one for, 'dork who lies around and eats too much fudge.'"

I think she's catching something from Sadie. How much do I have to ignore before I retaliate on these two?

"What are you maniacs doing out there?" Eric repeated. He pulled his pillow over his eyes.

"Shh, guys. Not so loud," Becky said. "We're going back down to the creepy people's tents and spy on them. I have a feeling Teya's doing something rotten and we are going to prove it."

"I'm going, too." I looked around for my shoes.

"Yeah, me, too," Eric mumbled from under his pillow. And his snores started again.

50

"No way, bro...you stay here," Sadie hissed. "We'll go down and see what's going on now and then I promise we'll come right back and tell you everything."

"All right. I'll go out on the front porch with my binoculars and keep a watch out from here. I'll blink my flashlight if I spot anything."

Becky giggled and said, "Ok, **Chinodin**."

Is 'Big Windbag' better than Fudge Breath? I don't think so.

I watched Sadie and Becky tiptoe down to the site. the big tent was glowing. It looked like someone inside was watching TV because of the occasional ghostly flickers. Moving shadows danced up and down against the bright tent. Becky went inside the tent and quickly ran back out with Teya right behind her. Becky ran past Sadie, barely avoiding her. Teya kept running and plowed right into Sadie.

Teya, the drama queen, screamed and fell to the ground. "Help! Help! I'm being robbed!" She cried and kicked as if she was a two-year-old having a tantrum. Sadie and Becky's long stretched shadows disappeared into the tent.

My curiosity was killing me. I knew the girls weren't taking anything, but Teya's angry screams were sure to bring someone to the site.

A moment later I jumped when I heard—"I'm going to kill her!" Sadie and Becky arrived, panting as if they'd run for miles and plopped down on the steps next to me. "I want to torture her and make her hurt so badly before she dies that she'll scream like that for eternity!"

"Shh, Beck, don't flip out, you'll wake Eric."

"But she's online, selling bones and artifacts from a grave!" Sadie yelped. "I think I'm going to help Becky injure her."

"Oh great! Where is the stuff coming from?" I knew they wouldn't be so angry without reason.

Sadie still puffed like a little steam train. She exhaled loudly and said, "Guess what? There is a huge pile of bones, some dried leathery-looking stuff, stone tools and pottery next to a digital camera, and she was on the computer looking at *Boogie Bob's Barterland*. She's so wicked and sneaky she must be some kind of monster!"

"And on top of that," Becky hissed, "there's an empty box of hair dye the same shade as her hair on the table next to her bed. I think she's in disguise. I saw a professional makeup kit in there too. Maybe she'll have some real bruises and a real black eye from me to cover up!"

"Shh. Somebody's coming to see why Teya screamed," I said. "Becky, did she recognize you?"

"Yep! I wanted her to see me and know that I'm investigating her."

"I don't think she saw me," Sadie said. "But I'll bet she saw stars when my foot happened to get in her way."

"Be sure to lock your door and windows tonight in case she returns the favor and sneaks up on you."

"Good idea. She'll probably try to crawl up the wall and into our window and suck our blood."

Sadie smacked Becky's arm and said, "Oooh! Don't say that! You're scaring me!"

"Well, Sadie, you can just squawk like a chicken at her and she'll leave."

"Look who's talking, **Chinodin**," Becky said. "You know Teya gives you the creeps, too."

"Ha-ha," Sadie laughed. "**Chinodin** is a great name, Becky."

Ugh, I don't think so. I like Fudge Breath better… after eating the fudge.

"Better lay low tomorrow, ladies. I'll dig my binoculars out and we'll watch them when they rise from their evil slumbers after lunch tomorrow."

"I'll be a peeping **Chinodin**, too," Becky said.

We watched as a man bent down and spoke to Teya. He helped her off the ground and walked with her into the bright white tent.

Sadie gagged and said, "Yuck, I hope whoever he is doesn't die from her venom. Hey, Beck, do you think she might be a black widow spider or a female rattlesnake in human form?"

"Yes," Becky said seriously, "I do. I'm not only locking our door, I'm putting a big chair in front of it."

CHAPTER TWELVE

BATTING PRACTICE

That night I tossed and turned like a pancake on Aunt Dodo's sizzling griddle. Eric's snores were so deafening I wrapped my pillow around my head to block out the sound. All the odd stuff going on down at the tent kept my mind whirling. I must have gone to sleep because I woke up when something brushed my hair. Klink, klink, flitter-flitter. I reached over and flipped the light on.

"A bat?" It zipped down into my face again and I swung at it. "Arrgh! There's a bat in here!" I heard the high-pitched faint E-E-E-E"- noise that was almost a sound, but mostly a feeling. A few seconds later, another bat flew in through the open window and dove at my head.

The screen was out and the window was wide open. When did that happen? It was closed when we went to bed.

I pounded on the wall next to my bed and yelled, "Eric, wake up! Bats! Bats! There are bats in here!"

Eric jumped up swinging his pillow. My legs tangled up in the blankets and I fell out of bed and cracked my head on the nightstand. The stars were so beautiful.

"Ooo, my head. What happened?" When I opened my eyes, I was on the floor and Mom had a cold compress on my head. A lot of strangers were standing in my room looking at me. "What did I do now?"

Sadie leaned over me and said in a spooky sounding voice, "Do you remember the bats, Jared?"

I couldn't figure out why she talking about bats? We weren't playing baseball. "No. What do you mean, bats?" Everything was blurry. "Somebody give me my glasses."

Eric wiggled his fingers in the air and made swooping motions. "Ooo, the bats that came in the window. Bats flying all over our room … Ooo."

Then I remembered. I grabbed a blanket and pulled it over my face, "Arrgh! Bats! Look out, Mom! There are bats in here! They'll bite you and give you rabies!"

"Hey, Jared… Fudge Breath, calm down," Becky yelled. "They're all gone. Eric chased them back outside."

"What is going on? Bats were all over the place in here. I saw Eric jump up and that's all I remember." I felt my legs. "Oh good, I have my pajamas on."

"Well, your dorkyness," Sadie could not stop giggling at me, "I heard you clear upstairs. You screamed and screamed, fell out of bed and scared everyone in the house out of a sound sleep. You cracked your skull on the nightstand and almost crushed Huron, who must have been under your bed. Mom called the doctor while you were unconscious and he says you might have a concussion."

"Oh great, a concussion. That's all I need. And Huron was under the bed? No wonder my nose kept running. So, what's next?"

Mom said, "I don't know. You'll be seeing the doctor tomorrow. We have to keep you awake for a few hours to make sure you're okay."

"Yahoo! Euchre time." I rubbed my hands together. "Get the cards. I've been waiting for a chance to beat someone."

"Okay, have fun, but please don't fall out of bed again." Mom took the compress with her and went back to bed.

"Aw, too bad, Fudge Breath. I hate cards and I have to work tomorrow," Eric said and ran for the door, swinging his batty pillow. "I'm going upstairs to sleep in the extra bed in the girl's room. He's all yours, Beck and Sade. Night."

"**Chinodin**, if you think you're going to beat me at cards, think again. I will massacre you," Becky said.

"Me, too," Sadie said. "Deal the cards."

"Oh, now I really have a headache. It must be fudge withdrawal."

56

It was a long, painful night. Every time I closed my eyes for a second I'd drift off. Then I'd see those snarling little ratty faces and yell, "Arrgh, Bats!" and Sadie would punch me until I woke up.

And they beat me at cards, too.

CHAPTER THIRTEEN

LOOK WHAT I DUG UP

After I saw the doctor and Mom found out I was okay, she broke the news to us.

"Aunt Dodo's doctor says she can get along without her wheelchair now, so June and Joe Redhawk asked me to go over to Mackinac Island to help them. They have a new store opening soon and they want me to the run the Gliding Wing Gallery for a week."

"A week? You are going to the island without us for a week?" I felt a huge disappointment.

"Yes. You'll survive without me. Aunt Dodo is not very good on steps yet and still needs your help. Jared, you will help the girls clean the upstairs rooms."

"Me, clean rooms?" I can't believe Mom was sticking me with the grossest job ever.

"You will clean the bathrooms."

"UGH! No way! I hate to clean bathrooms!"

Mom grinned at me and patted me on the head. "It has to be done. Aunt Dodo has plastic gloves for you to use. By the way, when we get home you will be cleaning our house a lot more."

"Mom! That is not fair!" Sadie and Becky were giggling so hard at me having to clean bathrooms that I wanted to throw something at them. "Cut out the laughing, you—women!"

"While the girls make the beds, vacuum and dust, you will clean the bathrooms. You all will help Aunt Dodo cook, do dishes and laundry. It's an even distribution of work since I did all the cleaning before now."

"But Mom, how am I supposed to study?" That report was still hanging over my head.

"You'll have evenings. When I come back, I'll help you get it in order."

"Please, Mom. Don't do this to me. I want to go to the island, too."

"You'll get your chance."

Ten minutes later, we walked her to the ferry and she was off to the island.

When we came back to the Inn, it was almost 11:00. I wanted a nap, but we had to work. Bummer! I have never cleaned so many rooms in my life. There was only one room we weren't allowed to touch. The sneezy man's room. I just put Mr. No Cats' clean towels on a bathmat next to his door and walked away.

On the way back to my room I yawned and said to Sadie and Becky, "What a long, long, day. I think I'm traumatized by all the work and Mom leaving us."

"What a dork!" Sadie squealed. "Work traumatizes you? Get over yourself, you big wimp!" and she booted me in the behind as she went upstairs.

Ahh, such is the life of a deprived child.

That night I slept like a rock and morning came all too soon.

Early the next morning I went to the dining room to get breakfast. Aunt Dodo and two other women were there drinking huge mugs of coffee, with a giant pile of lumpy biscuits on a tray in front of them.

"Morning." Aunt Dodo patted a chair. "Come join us and have some fry bread. Jared, this is my older sister and Luke's mother, Lulu La Croix, and this is my little sister, Rosie Bush. Don't tease her about her name because she's a hairdresser and you have an appointment for a haircut very soon." The blonde woman smiled at me and said, "Nice hair, Jared."

Becky sat down next to me and passed me the hot cocoa pot. "What's fry bread?" I asked. "I've never heard of it before."

"Indian bread. These are like beignets, French pastries from New Orleans." Becky dropped one on my plate. "Teya just told Aunt Lulu that the wedding is off for now because she discovered something in their back yard."

"Hey Aunties, are you going down to look at what Teya found?" Eric yelled from the front porch.

Aunt Lulu yelled back, "Yeah, I guess! Since it is in my yard!" She picked up her coffee mug, and grabbed another chunk. "Thanks, Dodo. This is almost as good as chocolate for fighting the blues."

No it isn't. Fudge is much better. But I grabbed a couple more for the road.

Eric yelled from the porch, "Hey, Jared. I'm heading down. Tell everybody to hurry up."

Eric, Becky, Sadie and I were at the site when the aunts caught up to us.

We joined some neighbors who were already inside the big white tent looking around. "What did they find?" I asked Becky, who was staring angrily at Teya.

Aunt Lulu yelled at Teya, "Why are white graves sacred and our Native graves not sacred! Close it up and leave it alone, girl!"

CHAPTER FOURTEEN

WHAT IS SACRED

That was a good question. I had to think about it for a while. Why are white graves so special that they are called sacred and not touched? Why are Native American graves not thought to be the same? Is it curiosity or lack of respect?

After a few minutes, all three aunts went into Lulu's house, and invited the neighbors in while the four of us stayed behind.

"Look!" Becky pointed into a neat square hole in the ground about four feet wide and five feet deep. "That skeleton is wearing beads that look like my wedding beads! But if they are really old the thread should have rotted and the string of beads should be in pieces. Teya, did you mess with my necklace?"

Teya had a heavy net over her wide brimmed hat. We could barely see her face. She glanced into the hole and didn't answer Becky for a minute. The she sneered, "No, little child, I don't even know what your precious beads look like."

"Whoo! Is it really a grave?" Ugh, spooky! I grinned down at the skull and the skull smiled back at me with very nice teeth. I wasn't an expert at all but something didn't seem right about the grave. It looked too clean and perfect. Something that old should be sort of crunchy-looking with rotted disgusting clothes and lumpy body leftovers. It didn't smell dead. It just smelled like dirt—clean dirt. Since meeting the flat squirrel, I know what dead smells like.

"What do you want, o' round one?" Up close Teya was beautiful, except for the sneer on her attractive lips and the evil squint in her brown eyes.

"Huh? What do you mean? I don't want anything. I'm looking at your skull's nice wig and that set of teeth. It's quite unusual for such an ancient grave, isn't it? I thought people had bad teeth back then."

Dude muttered, "How do you know, genius boy?"

I snorted rudely and said, "Duh… I read. They didn't use toothpaste in the past and there weren't any dentists either. They yanked the bad teeth out with no anesthesia. This guy or girl should have some major cavities and empty spots instead of perfect teeth."

Teya looked at me as if I had been dipped in fresh horse hockey. "Get out of my tent, you smart alec gordo. You were not invited anyway."

Hmm… gordo? So now, she's insulting me in Spanish?

"The name is Jared, not Gordon… Gordo is my second cousin once removed from Caro, Michigan." I refused to sink to her level. Every time she insulted me, she sounded more and more pathetic.

"Come on, calm down, Teya. I invited Jared to come down to celebrate your success," Eric said.

She looked past Eric and curled her lip. "My name is Dr. Dove!" She sneered at Sadie and me. "This is a private dig. I asked no one to come in here but my fiancé's family. You are not in his family, Eric. Get out and take the fat white ones with you!"

"Wait a minute, woman, that's ridiculous," Eric said. "Luke and I are both part of the Redhawk family. You aren't worth my time. I'm going up to eat breakfast," and Eric marched off.

Sadie ran up and stuck her fist in Teya's face. "What do you mean,fat? I'm not fat! I'm perfect for my height! And don't you talk about my best friends like that, you insulting bag of bones!" Sadie said. "I ought to…"

"Sadie!" I saw what she was planning and clamped my hand onto her shoulder. "NO! Don't do it! I promised Mom…." I yanked Sadie away and almost fell backwards trying to pull her with me.

Sadie tried to get away. She yelled, "But Jared, I want to pound her. She deserves it!"

"No!" I kept a tight hold on her shirt. "Mom said I wasn't to let you hit anyone or she'd tell Dad. You remember what happens then?"

Sadie gave me a cheesed off look and snarled, "Okay. Since I don't want to be grounded for the rest of my life, I can't pound her. You go get her, Beck!" I caught sight of Becky's face. It was the same shade of watermelon pink I had seen before when she was mad at me. She was furious and barely in control.

What is this? A tag-team shouting match?

Becky said, "Dr. Dove?"

Teya turned to look at Becky with her lip curled in an annoyed sneer. "What?"

Becky pointed at the skeleton. "That better not be my necklace in that fake grave or you will be in a lot of trouble. If this were a real grave, besides the necklace there would be a medicine bag on that skeleton."

Teya's expression changed as Becky mentioned the medicine bag. It went from a look of rude contempt to a quick look of excitement, then back to a sneer again. Something about medicine bags got her attention.

Becky never noticed the change in Teya; she just had to have her say. "Wait until Luke finds out that you are nothing but a scrawny whining liar! You are no more Native American than I am Chinese. By the way, these 'Whites' *are* part of my family. We have been through a lot together. We don't treat each other that way. Come on, family, let's go!"

When Becky stomped out of the tent, Sadie followed her. On my way out I turned around and said, "Oh, by the way, Dr. Dove. Enjoy your last look at the site. I'm going to call the state archeologist's office today."

Teya stomped her feet like a spoiled child having a tantrum. She screamed, "Oh! How dare you? How could you? You idiots! I should…. Arrgh! Get that stupid cat out of here!"

Crazy Huron must have followed us down the hill. He happily rolled on the dirt pile and played with something. I reached over and picked it up.

Sadie snorted rudely and said, "Come on out of there, Huron baby. It's probably poisoned food." She picked up the cat and carried it with her.

"Don't touch anything, you idiot!" Teya shouted. "It's not cataloged yet!"

"Whoa, I'm so scared! It's a pork rind, Teya. I'll take it with me because it would probably contaminate your fake grave. Nice tea staining by the way, but the bones aren't quite the right color."

I grinned and pocketed the pork rind. "I'll put it with the rest of my collection later."

I had to rub it in some more. "Hey Becky," I said, "do you think those bones might have DNA in them? Some polyethylene fake-o?"

"Yeah, she's a fake-o all right. I'll bet she isn't even a real archaeologist."

Teya screamed, "You wait!" She started toward us with a pointed trowel in her hand. "I'll fix you both!"

Dude jumped in front of Teya. He held his hand up in Teya's face and yanked the trowel from her hand.

"Stop it, Teya. You are out of control."

"Can't you do something?" she whined. When Dude shook his head no, she screeched, "I swear you're useless, Thomas!"

66

Dude shook his head again. "I'm useless? Did you get permits to dig? You told me you got permits from the city. We can't do anything if *you* didn't get permits."

"Leave this tent!"

"Aw, Come on, Teya. You don't really mean it! Where am I going to sleep?"

"I don't care!"

I didn't wait around any longer. I left to help with breakfast before the fight really got rolling.

CHAPTER FIFTEEN

BAD MEDICINE

That afternoon Sadie said it was time for my haircut appointment. She told me I looked like Huron and she didn't want to be seen with me anymore, so she dragged me to Aunt Rosie's hair salon for a trim.

I sat down in Aunt Rosie's shampoo chair, yanked off my baseball cap and my hair puffed up like a hot air balloon.

"Wow, Jared. Now that is a bunch of hair. If you wait a few months, you will have enough to donate to *Locks of Love* for a wig. Becky has one more inch to grow on her braids and she's going to cut them off. You only need to donate ten inches and you probably have half that now."

"What? Becky's cutting off her braids? She won't look right without them."

"Sure she will. Didn't Eric tell you he's cutting off his ponytail at the same time?"

"No way! Eric without a ponytail? He'll look strange."

"Maybe. But little kids who have lost their hair during cancer treatment will have free wigs because Eric and Becky donated their hair."

"Good idea. I'll let mine grow long over next winter. I'm too hot right now."

Aunt Rosie reminded me of her brother, Joe Redhawk, Becky and Eric's dad. When she smiled, her dimples showed up and her crinkly brown eyes almost disappeared. She teased me, "Well, what should I do with this shrub?"

"Take'er down. It will be back in two weeks. My hair grows like I use fertilizer for shampoo."

Half a dozen women laughed when they heard my goofiness.

Aunt Rosie combed through my hair and hit the spot that smacked the nightstand.

"Ouch!"

"You've got a whopper of a bruise. What happened?"

I said really fast, "Somebody put bats in our room last night and I got my feet tangled up in the blanket and fell out of bed trying to get away from them...."

Aunt Rosie's eyes got big. She whispered, "Bats in Dodo's house? That's awful! Don't tell anyone else. It will ruin her reputation in the bed and breakfast community and she'll lose a lot of money.

"We'll keep it quiet. Nobody will hear it from us."

"Lay back in the sink and I'll give the shrub a scrub."

As suds covered my head, someone ran past and smacked me. "Ouch! Is that Sadie?"

"Who else? Shh Jared, listen...." Sadie dropped down next to the shampoo bowl and whispered in my ear, "Guess who went back to the tanning rooms?"

I scooped the suds out of my ear with my finger. "Who? Frosty the snowman? Casper the Friendly Ghost? They could both use a tan."

Sadie blipped me on the nose.

"Ow! Cut it out!"

"Get serious, dork."

I couldn't roll my eyes because there was too much shampoo. "Believe me, I am. Tell me and stop torturing me when I'm helpless here."

She said, "Helpless? Ha." Then she whispered, "Teya the grave robber is tanning."

Aunt Rosie turned to look at the tanning room door. "Really? Now why would Dr. Dove need to tan? Archaeologists are outside all the time."

"I followed her part way back and peeked," Sadie said. "It's hot back there and when she took off her shirt, I saw that her skin is fish-belly white. She's lighter than I am with my red hair."

"Maybe she's getting a spray tan. We do those, too," Aunt Rosie said.

At the next station a tall black woman with blue streaks in her hair asked, "You talking about Miz *Doctah* Dove? She shore is a prissy one. She came in yesterday and wanted me to touch up her roots, but I had a full schedule. Said she'd find somebody else to do it. So I said, 'Go ahead.' and she left in a hurry."

"Roots?" I asked. "What kind of roots?"

"Well honey, she is a natural platinum blonde. Her real hair is almost pure white."

"Toldja so," Sadie giggled. "She must have colored her own hair yesterday. And she says she's full-blooded Ojibwa."

"If she's full Ojibwa, I'm a natural blonde moose's patoot." Aunt Rosie touched the tall stack of blonde curls on her head. "I don't think there are any full-blooded Ojibwa Indians in this area. Most everyone now is a mix of Ottawa, Ojibwa, French and a lot of the rest of the world. I think she's full of a lot of **Mudjimushkeeki**."

"Whoa, that sounds messy. What is it?" I asked.

Aunt Rosie shook her head sadly, "That means my nephew should stay far away from her because she is full of *bad medicine*."

CHAPTER SIXTEEN

REDHAWK'S EXCELLENT FUDGE

When I got back into the house five pounds lighter from my haircut, I recognized a guy with a ponytail relaxing on the front porch swing.

Sadie and Becky were hacking away at a poor beat up birdie during a two-girl badminton game. They screamed at each other like lunatics.

"You girls are going to wake the **Niboowin**!" Aunt Dodo yelled from the kitchen window. "We'll have spirits walking all over the place if you don't quiet down. Ten minutes until lunch. Hurry up and get in here!"

"Yay. I'm starved. You're back early," I said to Eric. "How did you escape?"

"Dad is training people today and he didn't need me, so I checked over the stable and came back to help Aunt Dodo out. This place is hopping with fudgies too, just like the island."

"Yeah, I wish I was one of them…the smell of that island is like fudge paradise. I can't wait for Mom to get back over here. I've been calling her but she never answers the phone. It seems like she's been gone for a week, but it's only been a day."

"Oh yeah, I forgot to tell you. Her cell phone went on the fritz and my mom says she'll be working at the Gliding Wing for two weeks."

"Two weeks? But we're only supposed to be here for two weeks total. Now that the wedding has been postponed, I thought we'd be heading home…not that I really want to. I hope she sent some fudge money back. I need, I crave…I have to go to the fudge store—she promised!"

"No fudge cash. But I brought you this." Eric handed me a big white bag with a flying red bird on the side and yanked a wad of cash out of his pocket. "And this cash is from your mom to pay Aunt Dodo with."

"What is it?" I pocketed the money, held up the sack and shook it.

Eric couldn't stop smiling. "I thought you liked to read. Open it and see."

I read the sack, "'Redhawk's Gourmet Fudge'. Wow! This bag must weigh ten pounds. O' Great Pony Tail, I am not worthy!"

"Yep. All for you, FB. I'd rather shovel horse manure, but I've been learning how to make fudge. Since your mom runs the Gliding Wing Gallery now, my mom and dad are slinging lots of fudge."

"Whoopee! It's Pony Tail?" Sadie flew up the steps, jumped on Eric's back and wrapped her arms around his neck.

I had the sack open and my face buried in it, smelling the fudge, absorbing it, becoming one with it. I crackled the bag, never removing my face from it. "Look, Sadie."

"Redhawk's Fudge? Mmm. Is it good?"

"Ack, Sadie, you're strangling me! Let go!" Eric peeled Sadie off his back and dropped her on the porch table. "Couldn't tell anyone about the new store. Dad found some new recipes, like chocolate caramel bacon fudge, and chocolate potato chip fudge, and cherry fruitcake fudge. He always makes odd pizzas so he decided to make strange fudge flavors. Store was a secret until yesterday when we opened. We don't even have our sign up yet, but, yowsers, we have a lotta fudge. My arms are killing me from scraping the fudge around on the marble slab. But I got paid."

"Cool." Sadie grinned from her perch on the table. "You know Jared won't share that bag of fudge, don't you?"

"Yep. Here's your bag, and a little gift from another store." Eric handed Sadie a bag the same size as mine and a little pink sack with a pair of made-up eyes on the front.

Sadie peeked inside the pink bag, "Wow, that's a lot of make-up."

Eric laughed, "Yeah, the store was going out of business and I remembered how you like make-up. You don't need it, though. You look nice without it."

Sadie smiled, "Okay, Pony Tail, I'll save it and take it home. Do you mind if I share it with my friends?"

Eric pretended to put lipstick on. "Since it looks bad on me, it's all yours. Ouch!" Sadie whacked him and reached into her fudge sack. "Any coffee or mocha flavors in here?"

Becky wandered around in the front yard, looking lost. "Rats," she grumbled. "Where did I drop my book? Yo bro, how're the old folks doing?"

"Great. Store's open. I'm sick of fudge. Brought you a surprise. The Tome Tomb had a really great sale and I found these."

"*Ojibwa Songs and Legends,* and *Dictionary and Phrases of the Ojibwa Language,* Whaa-hoo!" Becky bounced all around the porch as if she had springs on her shoes. "Now I don't have to buy them myself."

"Half price." He tossed another bag at Becky. "Have some fudge to ruin your lunch, but keep it away from me."

"Last call for lunch!" Aunt Dodo yelled. And the girls ran inside.

"Come here, Fudge Breath, I need to talk to you, but please don't breathe on me."

I stood back a foot or so. "Yum-Kay," I managed to say around a bite of the creamy maple chocolate chunk fudge. "Wass-up?"

"Dad says the Fort De Buade museum's back door was open a couple of times in the morning when the staff came in. Nothing is missing, but they're painting and re-setting some displays, so it's a little confusing down there.

"Do you think someone is returning stuff from the museum to its original owners again, like Luke did on the island?"

"Naw. The things in this museum were purchased or donated a long time ago. They don't have any bones or grave items that should be re-buried."

I had to ask. "Do you think Luke sent Teya here?"

Eric got this tough look on his face. "I don't know, but something is not right about her visit."

"NOW! You boys get in here right now!" Aunt Dodo ordered.

"Careful, Aunt Do," I laughed. "You'll raise the **Niboowin**!"

"Okay. You two are washing all the pans for the next two days," she said.

"No! Not the pans!" Eric moaned. "It's all your fault, Fudge Breath."

CHAPTER SEVENTEEN

A COFFIN?

It took me several hours of staring at that hearse from the twenty bathrooms I scrubbed before I actually got up the guts to investigate it. I knew I shouldn't do it, but I had to see what was in the back of Dude's car. That car was too strangely beautiful to be just an old hearse, and the words on the side had to be some kind of clue to what was inside. I thought I'd take a hike and see what was going on.

Dude crawled out of the car. Or should I say slithered out in his red satin outfit, and went into the house. My curiosity was worse than Huron's. And my big toe was sore from Huron's curious nibbles in the middle of the night.

Thinking about that cat made my nose twitch. "Ker-Choo!"

Somewhere in the house, I heard a loud sneeze echo me. "Wa-choo!"

I started walking down the hill.

"Hey, Fudge Breath! Where you going?" Eric yelled from the attic window.

"Darn, I can't sneak up on anything! I guess I'm going nowhere."

"Wait up." Eric galumphed down the interior steps and vaulted down five steps to the ground.

"Show off," I muttered.

"I know you're up to something. I can see it in those baby blue peepers of yours."

"No I'm not."

"Yes, you are. It can't be a fudge attack; I brought you a ton of fudge."

"Look, Pony Tail, I'm going to take a stroll."

"Yeah, I get it—down the hill to the tents and that shiny red target with wheels that's yelling at you 'Come and get me. I'm hiding something from you. You know you want me.' Hee hee hee."

"So?" I kept walking down the sidewalk.

"So, you know, Dude is strange enough to make me curious, too. So, let's go."

"What happens if he sees us?"

"Kill him with kindness and beg to get a closer look. He'll let us see it. I can tell he's proud of it."

"Why would I want to do that? They don't like me and the feeling is mutual."

At the bottom of the hill where the sidewalk ended, we took a left. The gate was open and Dude's car keys were within reach.

"Get the keys," I whispered as I pretended to walk past.

Eric squatted down and walked like a crab into the yard.

People were talking inside the house. I hoped nobody was looking out the back door. I kept walking and whistled loud and off key. With all the noise I made, I hoped they'd see me and not Eric.

"Got em," Eric whispered and ran to the back of the hearse.

I turned around and tried to sneak back to the car. When I turned, I tripped over something and fell flat on my face in the gravel road.

"Ouch! That was dumb."

"Cool," Eric whistled. "Wowser! Come here. You gotta see this."

"I'm coming! It's going to take a minute."

"What's the matter? You okay?" Eric shut the door and came over to me.

"Yeah, just wiping off the blood. I tripped and tried a little experimental plastic surgery on my schnozz." We headed back up hill to the Inn.

"Must be the big feet."

"Yeah, tell me about it. I'm like a semi- truck in a Volkswagen world."

"That's very true. Or Big Bird in a nest of sparrows…"

"Enough already— what was in there?"

"I couldn't see much. But there were CD's. Ton's of them. Racks and racks."

"CDs? But why?

"Don't know, man. But, wowsers, there was a bunch. There was something else, too." *Wowsers* must be Eric's word this summer.

"What?" I hoped there'd be something more exciting than a bunch of CD's.

"A coffin."

I guess I was expecting something like clothes or something from Teya's site. I wasn't expecting to hear the word *coffin*. I stopped in my tracks. "Huh? For real? A coffin? You're joking, right?

"Nope, man…it looked like a real regulation wooden coffin with shiny gold trim, sitting on a big metal base."

CHAPTER EIGHTEEN

LOOK INSIDE, IT'S AN EMPTY CAN

I heard through the grapevine that Dude was going to Mackinac Island for the rest of the day. That meant we could check out that beautiful red bomb again.

Eric and I went down and hung around the park. Of course, Teya was nearby puttering around inside the tents, but when she left, I grabbed Dude's keys from the picnic table, opened the car and bailed into the driver's seat and Eric jumped into the passenger side. To our surprise, there wasn't a seat or seatbelt, only wooden boxes to sit on. Even the carpeting was gone. So much for riding in style.

I turned around to check the back. Instead of a view of the coffin and a place to climb into, there was a solid metal wall with a big crack up the middle.

"Wowsers," Eric said, "it looks so good on the outside but it's hollow on the inside. This car gets stranger and stranger."

Next to the speed dials on the dash, there was a panel with lights, labeled buttons, and slots with sliding buttons. Eric read, " 'Reverb, treble, track balance, speaker 1, speaker 2, audio, mic 1, mic 2, feedback, distortion, hi, mid range, track echo, output, phono, tape, CD.' This doesn't make any sense. Is this car a sound board or a big synthesizer?"

I was totally confused. "All right, *now* we have to look in the back again."

Eric looked past me and his eyes bugged out of his face. When his ponytail started vibrating he yelled, "Duck! It's Teya!"

"Don't worry. She can't see us through these dark windows."

His eyes got bigger. "But, she's coming this way carrying something. She has keys and she's going to open the door!"

I gave him a shove toward the passenger door, "Move it! Get out your side and I'll follow you."

Eric threw the passenger door open and rolled onto the ground. I was right behind him, but I got caught between the control panel and the four speed shift. By the time I fell out the door, Eric was hiding in the bushes. I shut the door quietly but I was afraid to latch it. I lay in the dirt next to the car trying not to pant like a winded puppy. I felt the car move. I knew she was going to catch me if she climbed into the car because the door was still partly open.

"Hey, Teya. What 'cha doing?" I heard Eric said casually. "It looks like you've been busy."

"What do you want and why do you care?" I couldn't see her but I could hear the sarcasm in her voice.

Eric said, "Trying to be a friend to my new cousin-to-be. Let me carry that box. It looks heavy."

As I started crawling for the bushes, I heard a slight scuffle. Eric said, "Calm down, Teya. I'm trying to help you."

Teya yelled, "No! Give it back! You aren't going to be my cousin, and it's none of your business what I have."

"But it's heavy. I'll set it here while you open the car. Ooh, it rattles...."

"No! Give it back to me!"

Eric had her confused and angry, so I pushed the door shut until it latched. Then I rolled away from the car and hid behind a tree.

I heard him shake the box one more time.

"Hmm. Sounds like gravel or dried beans. Let me peek... Hmm, that's interesting lumpy stuff."

I heard a slap. "No! Leave it alone. Get away from me before I call the police and have you arrested for... something."

"Oooh! Was that a love tap? I know- why don't you go out with me? We can go up to the Soo and watch a movie."

She screeched, "What? You're a... baby. Get lost."

"Hey, I'm sixteen. I'm not a baby." I heard him give the box one last shake. "Here. It's all yours. Can't you take a joke, Doc? ..."

"Humph. And don't call me 'Doc', you irritating child."

Eric walked my way. "Stay there," he mumbled. "She's hot like fire, man."

I heard a click and the car door locked. She struggled with the hatch door.

"Unlocked? Why was this car left unlocked?" Teya fumbled with the keys. Soon she yanked the rear door open, shoved the box in, slammed the door, and stalked away.

"Thomas! You left the car unlocked."

Dude was back?

"Nah, I'm sure I locked it," Dude yelled.

"Well then somebody has been messing with it. You better keep an eye on these strange people around here."

I was ready to run for the Inn when I heard, "Psst!" I about jumped out of my shorts.

"It's official," Eric said. "They have some weird stuff in that box."

"What did it look like?"

"A blackened section of a spine, and some rotten old medicine bags."

"Ugh. Who'd want that?"

CHAPTER NINETEEN

ATTACK CAT ON PATROL

I was up late working on my paper and had just gone to sleep, when I felt like someone was holding my head down and had stuffed something fuzzy in my mouth. I was choking and wheezing. I couldn't breathe.

"Cat! Will you get off my face?" I shoved him onto the floor. "How did you get in here?"

At three in the morning, the town of St. Ignace is very quiet. I had to get some air and get away from that puffball cat who loves me.

Our room was the first window by the front door and overlooked the porch. I took a blanket, a glass of water, and my asthma inhaler, went out the front door in my pajamas and curled up on the porch sofa. I had my eye on one tent in Aunt Lulu's back yard that glowed like the brightest full moon I had ever seen. There were some super bright lights on inside.

I think I fell asleep for a while, when I heard a WHAM that woke me straight up. In the radiance that lit the street next to the tent, I saw something move. Grabbing my glasses, I saw Teya trudging back to the tent from a dumpster in the back of the hardware store. I didn't know if I could wait until morning to find out what she put in there. She stopped and looked toward me. I froze in place, hoping she couldn't see me. I noticed the light in Eric's and my bedroom had come on and it was right next to where I was sitting.

"Shhh!" I hissed. "Hey Eric, turn off the light."

"Who's out there? 'S-zat you, Fudge Breath?"

"Shh, Teya's up to something."

"Kay- man. Thought I heard something. Be out in a sec." The bedroom light went out and Teya dashed back into the tent.

"'Cha doing out here?" Eric arrived so quickly and quietly I almost yelped.

"Whoa. Did you walk through a wall or something?" I asked.

"Nah, I crawled out the window."

"Oh. I didn't know it opened."

"Yeah, all the screens come off," he said. "What's going on?"

"Huron tried to sleep on my face so I came out here for air. Then Teya dumped something in the hardware store trash bin and woke me again."

"Sooo? What do you want to do?" Eric rubbed his blinky eyes.

"Go look in the trash bin."

A large yawn attacked him and he plopped onto the sofa. "Why? It's the middle of the night and I need to sleep."

I thought hard while the shining tents called to me.

86

"Yeah, yeah, I know. But you have to wake up so you can pull their plug. Then while they're scrambling around in the dark, I'll be looking in the trash to see what made so much noise. It has to be something big or she would have shoved it into a crack and not lifted the lid so high."

"Good idea, Fudgie, but I think you should pull the plug and I should look into the trash and rescue the item. Then we'll have less drama, because I occasionally take the big trash pieces out for Aunt Dodo. No one will suspect me of doing something sneaky if I carry trash out at night. You look totally sneaky all the time. Ouch!" Eric jumped and shook his leg like it was on fire. "Back off, Huron! I didn't insult Jared. I stated an opinion."

I had to laugh. Huron was wrapped around Eric's leg, chewing on his calf. "Sic 'em, Huron! Okay, tell me where the plug is located and give me a few minutes."

To avoid Huron's sharp teeth, Eric picked the cat up and held him close. He pointed to the yard. "Do you see where the orange cord goes into the right corner of the tent? If you follow it back about three feet, you can unplug it there."

"Okay. I'm heading out."

"Hey, FB?"

"Yeah?"

"Mind the tent stakes and ropes. They'll get you."

"Tent stakes and ropes? Okay. I will mind them."

I snuck quietly down the hill. The tent lights glowed blue-white in the dark night and soft rock music played on the radio. I slunk past, found the cord and followed it.

"Okay here goes."

"Mrow?"

"Huron!" I hissed. "Why are you following me? S-s-s! Get away!" The cat jumped onto my bent back and sat there like a lawn ornament.

"Get off!" I hissed and shook my shoulders. Huron dug his toenails into my back and hung on. I reached back and pushed him.

"Mrow-owow," the crazy cat landed on the grass with a thump.

I heard voices and digging and scraping sounds in the tent. I figured it was now or never. I yanked the two cords apart. Instant blackness. I waited to see what would happen next, because I was completely blind.

"My computer! The light! What happened to the electricity? I can't work without a light!" Teya screamed, and Dude answered her. "I don't know. Maybe it's a power failure."

"I should have expected this creepy little backwoods town to be this way. We have to get this work done and get out of town. Climb out of that hole and find a flashlight! Then look outside and see if anyone else in town is out of power."

"Yes, your highness," Dude grumbled. I heard a loud smack like someone hit someone else. "Hey, cut it out! I didn't cause the outage."

"Well, you deserved it. This mess is all your fault," Teya shouted.

"Cool it, sis. It isn't my fault. You are just looking for someone to blame. I can't help it if you're running out of cash and your old boyfriends are hassling you."

"I only need a few more days and then we can get out of here. Those men are so irritating. One is a… temporary problem and the other is…. ugh. Never mind. They aren't my boyfriends. I hate them both!"

"Whoa. Two boyfriends? And she hates them both?" I wonder if Luke knows she hates him?

As interesting as Teya's words were, without the tent light I had no idea where I was or which way to go. I thought the road I came down was on the right…. or did I turn around when she yelled and I stopped to listen?

I dropped to my knees and crawled to the right. "Mrow?"

"Huron?" A tail whipped past my nose. I grabbed the tail and Huron tugged away and came back. I doubted if Huron would ever be my guide cat. My nose tickled at the thought of him touching me. I rubbed my dripping nose but it wouldn't stop running.

I hissed, "Go home, you silly cat."

My eyes started adjusting to the lack of light. I looked around and saw a distant light and reflection down in the harbor. I decided I'd better go in the opposite direction. I rubbed and pinched my nose until it hurt, but the awful itching kept on growing.

I heard someone coming closer and tried to hurry. "Ouch!" I hit a tent rope and knocked my glasses sideways. I grabbed them, turned left and cracked my head on a split-rail fence and poked my face into a spiky hedge. I crawled under the fence and buried myself as deep as I could in the bushes and prayed my tickling nose would quit.

I heard footsteps and heavy breathing. Then an exclamation, "Found it!" When the light came back on, I was surprised by its brightness. I lay there for a minute trying to figure out how I was going to get out of the bushes without someone seeing me.

"Somebody pulled the plug," Dude yelled at Teya. Then a half second later I heard, "Mrow?"

Then Dude yelled, "Ouch!" as Huron attacked him. "It's Aunt Dodo's cat from the inn! Leave me alone, cat!"

Get him, Huron, baby! I thought from my damp spot in the leaves. Then Dude ran back into the tent with Huron chasing him.

Crazy cat Huron saved me. I crawled over to the road, jumped to my feet, and ran back up the hill as fast as I could. I even forgot to sneeze. I had to laugh as I remembered Dude running away from Huron.

"Hey FB." I jumped as Eric hissed from the porch. "You will never guess what was in the trash bin."

"What?"

"A skeleton."

CHAPTER TWENTY

A SKELETON?

I heard him, but I wasn't sure I completely understood him. "Really? You're kidding me."

"Sorta. It's a box from a skeleton kit. The kind they hang in the biology room at school."

"I was bugging Teya to irritate her but that skeleton down in the hole was too perfect. So I was right, huh?"

"Don't know, man. There's a scrap of a note in the box. Faint writing. I can't read it." Eric poked his flashlight closer to the note. "'No one will ever know.' Wonder what that means."

"I overheard Dude and Teya. She has two boyfriends. Teya said one was a temporary problem and one she said 'Ugh,' and didn't want to talk about. She said she hated them both."

"Whoa. Wonder which one Luke is? Maybe I should ask Dude a few careful questions."

"Well, she did decide not to marry him," I said. "Do you think Luke and Aunt Lulu are being used for some reason?"

"Yeah." He stared downhill. "Hey, shut the light off. I saw someone in the bushes coming this way." Eric shoved the box through the open window and dove in behind it.

"Get out of the way —I'll coming, too!"

The window was too narrow for me, so I slid down between the sofa and chair and pulled my blanket over my head. Maybe whoever it was would think I was a beanbag chair. I heard heavy wheezing breaths and stealthy crunching footsteps coming closer and closer. A loud whisper slithered out of the night, "I have been watching you. I saw you .... I will get you." Someone was planning my death.

I couldn't help it—I gasped for air and tried to think of a way to get away from the voice. I had my flashlight but I didn't know where the voice was coming from. I was burning up under the blanket and my was heart pounding so loud I was sure whoever was after me could hear it, too.

"Hissssst! Rowl!" Huron howled and growled as if he was facing his worst enemy. "Mrow? Mrrooww-wow! Grr-wowl-wowl-wowl."

"Aie! Allez cat!" the scratchy voice yelled, "Get back, animal!" I heard running footsteps fade away down the hill.

I almost giggled. I have an attack cat standing guard. Maybe having him close by is almost worth the wheezing. I wiggled around until I pushed the chair aside and sat back down on the sofa.

I reached out to pet Huron when he came back. "Nice attack, kitty."

Huron jumped on my hand and clung like a sandbur with his claws and teeth. "Ow! Go away and let me sleep. I'll give you a big treat tomorrow." I grabbed my stuff, hurried inside and locked the door. Morning wouldn't come soon enough for me.

CHAPTER TWENTY-ONE

COMPRENEZ-VOUS LE FRANCAIS?

The next morning came way too early. When Sadie banged on my door to wake me up to help with breakfast, I was so tired I couldn't see straight. But Aunt Dodo served warmed sweet cherries and syrup and whipped cream on her famous malted waffles and that made getting up all worthwhile.

The bright red cherries made me think about the beautiful Boney Collector. Yes, that hearse looked as tasty as cherry pancakes, but cherries have pits and we found a few in Dude's car.

I spent most of the morning scrubbing the dining room and kitchen floors. I couldn't figure out why the inside of the hearse was made that way. When I finally hit the front porch for a break, I saw the tents I had visited the night before had been moved.

It looked like the fence between La Croix's house and Marquette Park was gone. I wasn't just shocked, I was blown away. I sat for at least a minute trying to figure out how and why they'd do that. It didn't add up. A person can't take over a public park.

As usual, Eric was going off to work. I stopped him as he was going out the door heading for the ferry.

"Yo, Ponytail. Am I seeing things? What do you see at the La Croix's house?"

"Huh? Did they set up the tent in the park?"

"Yep. And here I thought I had broken my glasses."

"Time to visit the city clerk's office."

"I'll go down as soon as I can. I'm assistant chef today so I don't know what time I'll make it."

It was much later in the day when the girls and I headed into town. Every time I passed the dig, it just made me wonder why it was so important. Everything they needed to know would be in the library or the State Archaeologist's office. All they had to do was ask.

On our way downtown, Becky decided we needed to see St. Anthony's Rock, an enormous rock almost as big as a house, standing up in the middle of a parking lot.

Sadie scratched her head. "What did they put it up here for? It would have been better down by the water."

Becky laughed and whapped Sadie. "Sadie, nobody put it here—it's always been here. It's a sea stack. The same kind of rock as Castle Rock on the mainland and Sugar Loaf and Arch Rock on the island."

"Ohh, I thought it was supposed to be some kind of monument. Duh. Now I feel really dumb."

"Nah, I should have told you about it before. They say people used it for band concerts about a hundred years ago. The band sat way up on the top and people sat down here to listen."

I thought about our band at home. "Fast way to lose a band director. If they were excited and waved their arms too much or took one wrong step backward, they would be airborne. You can't fly with a baton no matter how hard you wave it."

"Funny, Jared. Ha ha. Let's go."

Becky led the way down to the museum. "I want to stop here for a while. You and Sadie go on down to the Municipal Building and come back for me when you're done."

"Okay. Back soon."

When we got to the municipal building it looked like it was closed, but when I pulled on it, the door was open. We decided to see if anyone was still in the clerk's office. When we got upstairs, the lights were on and a man was looking in a filing cabinet.

"Hello? Are you open?"

The man jumped when Sadie spoke, but the scared look on his face turned to recognition. He backed away and held some papers up so I couldn't see his face.

I didn't know who he was, but he knew us. I felt kind of creeped out.

"*Allo*? 'Ow may I *aide*…err… 'elp you?" The man had a strong French accent.

"We are checking on an archaeological dig site. The one at Marquette Park?"

"*Oui*? It is … *parfait*. Just fine…is superb. I was just looking for myself. I have the … *formes* right here." He waved his handful of papers at us.

I said, "We were concerned that they were too close to the burial site."

"*Non*, is *merveilleux*. They can dig anywhere…" The man waved us to the door. "I am closing now… *bonsoir*. Good evening."

"All right." I looked at Sadie and she looked at me as we left the office.

"Weird man…" she said.

I peeked back into the office and saw the man digging again in the files. Papers were scattered everywhere.

"Do you recognize him?" Sadie whispered.

"No, but he sure knew us. Let's go before he sees us peeking at him."

A man in a guard's uniform was coming up the stairs and grabbed Sadie. "Hey, what are you kids doing in here? The building is closed."

"You are? I'm sorry. We were at the clerk's office and we're leaving now," I said.

"Wait a minute. Stand over there by the wall. How do I know you haven't stolen something?" the man in the guard's uniform said.

We backed up a little but didn't go to the wall. "The front door was open and the lights were on when we came in. Besides, what would we steal? It's just offices."

"Offices where they take money," the man leered at Sadie and rattled a pair of handcuffs. He leaned closer and tried to intimidate her. "Are you sure you haven't taken any money, little girl?"

"I don't have any of your dumb money," Sadie shouted.

"Hey! Leave her alone! She's a little kid." His face got mean, and his big nose turned red when I yelled at him.

"If you're so interested in people stealing things, you'd better go look at the clerk's office. Look! The man who was in there is leaving right now." Sadie pointed down the hallway behind us.

The guard acted as if we were trying to distract him, but he finally looked down the hall. He jerked in surprise. "Hey! What are *you* doing in there?" The guard barreled down the hall after the French-speaking man.

"Go, Sadie, go!" and we went down the steps and out the front door as fast as we could run.

CHAPTER TWENTY-TWO

THE VOICE AND THE UNVEILING

After our visit to the clerk's office, I didn't feel any better. Why did the Frenchman know us and we had no idea who he was? Why did the guard act like he knew the man in the clerk's office?

A while before sunset, I borrowed Uncle Bushy's fishing pole to catch some perch from the dock. Eric was back on the island scraping fancy fudge around on the marble slabs. I missed our old Mackinac Island fishing trips on Round Island. It felt like I never had a minute to myself during the day.

On my way to the dock I walked past the largest tent and heard something that made me stop and listen.

"No! No!" Teya yelled, "I won't do it." And then I heard a crash as something large fell over.

"*Ecoutez*! Listen to me, Teya. Are you listening to me?" the hoarse voice scratched out.

It sounded as if the person talking had a French accent, but I couldn't tell if it was a man or woman. Was it the same person we met in the clerk's office?

"Yes, I'm listening." Her high voice suddenly sounded very strained. "Please. I can't breathe and... my necklace... you're cutting me... please don't break it. All right. I'll do what you want."

"You are not work... fast enough. *Mon temps*...my time is important. You aren't delivering what you promised. Do you understand?"

"Ow! Please don't hurt me. I'm doing my best."

"Does your *frere*, brother know?"

"He doesn't know anything. I'll collect your precious old bones and garbage, but you leave him alone!"

The voice quavered, "You're becoming a *petite princesse* for such a loathsome being, aren't you, Miss Vampire?"

A slapping noise and Teya cried out, "Vampire? Don't call me a vampire! You are a far more hideous creature than I am. You would drain the blood from your own children. I despise you! I wish you hadn't found me. Get out!"

An eerie giggle. "*Voyez-vous* Teya, my lovely *mystérieux fille*."

"I am not your daughter. Leave!"

"Oh, but you are. My superior blood definitely runs in your veins. You will do whatever I say or I will forget our deal. I can remove your dear brother Thomas from your life permanently. He is not yet eighteen and would love France. *Bonne nuit*."

Goose bumps rose up on my arms. I jumped behind the hedge and peeked around the bushes. I tried to see the person who was talking to Teya, but they were gone. I got a creepy feeling when I spotted a bat flying around Aunt Lulu's chimney.

Nah...couldn't be.... Or could it? Then I heard Teya crying.

I went over to the tent. What did I have to lose? All she could do to me was attack me, suck my blood, and turn me into a vampire, too.

I almost ran away and then reality struck me. "Wake up, Daly. Those kinds of vampires aren't real."

Teya sat on a cot near the door blotting her neck with a cloth.

"Teya? Are you okay?

"What? Oh, it's you, **Chinodin**. Get out of my tent! I don't have time to argue with you."

"I heard you crying."

"It's nothing but a small cut. See." She took the cloth from her neck. A bruise and an angry red line of blood notched into her neck.

"What happened?" It looked like someone tried to strangle her with a wire or cut her with something.

"Why do you care? I walked into a tent support rope and it scraped me."

"Oh. I've done that before. It hurt and made me feel kinda dumb, too."

"Yeah, I should have known that rope was so high," she said. "Now don't go telling everyone I was strangled or something, okay? Or I'll make you wish you'd never met me."

How did she know I didn't already feel that way?

She lifted her dark glasses and rubbed her eyes. Where I expected to see dark brown eyes, I was surprised to see pink watery eyes with pale blue irises stare at me like sad little bunny eyes.

"What happened to your eyes?" I gasped.

"What's the matter? Haven't you ever heard of colored contacts?"

"Yes, but I didn't think you wore them."

"Yes... the bright sun hurts my eyes."

"But why...?"

She jerked her head up and stared angrily at me. "Go away, Big Wind. You irritate me. I can't explain everything to you. Now get out of my face before I call a cop to arrest you!"

She irritated me, too. "Look, I want to help you. Don't try to scare me with a cop. My dad's a cop for the governor. I can pick up a phone and call him anytime. So don't threaten me with a cop."

I picked up her necklace from the tent floor and dangled it in her face. The clasp was broken.

"Hmm. Is this the tent rope you ran into? Better go hook it back out there before the tent falls down." I tossed the necklace into her lap. "You need to end this dig and ask the police to stop that French guy from bothering you. Is he your father? If he is, he sounds dangerous the way he threatened you and Dude."

As I walked away, she started crying again.

I spent a lot of time on my Marquette paper that evening. I thought it was almost finished, but it was so boring I knew I was going to get a rotten grade.

That night I tossed and turned and thought, *Are Teya and Dude really vampires like the voice said. Or are they Wendigos, like Becky thinks?*

I didn't know I had fallen asleep when I heard a whisper, "Jar-ed?" and a *tap, tap, tap* on my open window.

"What? Are you girls goofing around again? Go to bed." I got up, went to the window without putting my glasses on, and pulled the curtain aside. The screen was gone so I leaned slightly out the window. "Who's out there?"

A big hairy hand attached to a very strong arm grabbed my shirt and yanked me forward. My nose and forehead smashed into the upper window glass and frame. Through the cracked glass, I saw something from my worst nightmares. A ghostly lipless face with huge fangs snarled, "Do not go to de tents, or I will ahh...eat you!"

Then the hand shoved me and I landed with a thump on the floor. I was so shocked I couldn't move or speak. After I calmed down, I stumbled into the bathroom. I didn't want to ruin Aunt Dodo's towels so I ran cold water over my undershirt and held it to my bloody nose. I crawled into bed and pulled the covers over my head. I refused to believe it was a real Wendigo. Someone was trying to scare me.

CHAPTER TWENTY-THREE

THE PURPLE NOSE OF MACKINAC

I woke up early with painful memories of the night visit. I looked in the mirror and felt my purple nose very carefully. It felt like it was broken. My battered forehead was going to be purple, too. I looked out the open window. It was real. My window screen was across the yard and there was a huge crack in the window glass where my face had met it.

Whoever was making my life miserable was not going to get away with it anymore. I thought everyone was still sleeping, but I heard puttering in the kitchen. I stuck a piece of tape on the front door bell clapper so it wouldn't jingle when I went out the door and snuck out with Huron following behind me like a security-cat.

The window screen had been thrown like a Frisbee about fifty feet away from the Inn. When I picked it up there were white smudgy fingerprints all over it. That was my first real clue that it wasn't a ghoul who grabbed me. Ghosts do not have fingerprints.

I carried the screen back to my window. When I stepped onto the front porch, I saw a full handprint in white goopy stuff on the window edge. Does this guy have a brain? Either he thinks no one will check on him or he's crazy and doesn't care.

I reached into the open window, carefully laid the screen on the floor and headed downhill to the tents. I needed to talk to Dude and find out for myself if he could possibly be the Wendigo.

"Yo, Dude, are you in the tent?"

A sleepy voice yawned and said, "What do you want, Chubbo? Why are you up so early?" Dude yawned and stretched when he opened the tent flap. Then he jerked with surprise and stared at my face. "Who hit you?"

"You tell me." I think he could tell I was angry.

Dude looked amazed. "What are you talking about?"

"Come up to the Inn with me. I want to show you something."

He gave me a nervous look. "Okay...if you say so. Let me get dressed."

We hiked up to Partridge's in time for breakfast, but I was too angry to eat.

"Come in here." I shut the bedroom door behind us. Huron hopped onto the bed.

"Hey, man. What's going on? I don't know what you are up to, but I really am a good guy."

I picked the screen up and pointed to the edge. "White greasy fingerprints." I took him to the window. "White greasy hand print. Now show me your hands."

He held his hands up. I looked at both sides and checked his stubby fingernails. There wasn't a speck of white makeup anywhere.

"Ehh, your fingers are longer than the prints on the screen, anyway."

"Does this have anything to do with your nose?"

"Yep. I had a visit from a Wendigo last night. He told me to stay away from the tents and if I didn't, he was going to eat me."

"A what? What's a wen…?" Dude stared at me with those strange white eyes. "I don't know who is weird enough to want to eat you, but it not me."

"A Wendigo is a Native American cannibal…"

Dude's hand went up. "Stop right there. I have been called some strange things before but I've never been called a Wed…ni…go."

"Wen-di-go!"

"Look man, I don't know what they are! I've never heard of them before so get off my back!"

"All right, I believe you." I was getting nowhere with him. "Now stop calling me Chubbo!"

"Deal man. No more name calling."

"Will you keep your eyes open for strange people hanging around?"

"Huh?" He made a face and pointed to me. "You look like a very weird person and you hang around our site all the time."

I gave him a peeved look. "I am not weird! I'm bruised! Look Dude, I'll buy your breakfast today if you keep me informed if anyone unusual visits the dig site."

"Sold. I'm hungry."

Huron followed us into the breakfast room and we sat down at the big table. Sadie sauntered in carrying a big dish of scrambled eggs. "Mmm, coffee's done! I want big cup of java—Dude, why are you here?"

"Mornin'. Food!" He raised his half-empty juice glass toward her. The pile of food on his plate was higher than mine was.

I hid my face with my hand and a piece of toast.

"Good morning. Dig in. Aunt Dodo has the morning off so Becky cooked this morning." Sadie shot me a surprised look as Dude shoveled in his food like a starved person.

She reached down to pet Huron. "Come here Huron baby-cat and let me hold you." Then she did a perfect double take. "Wow! What happened? You and Eric have an argument and your nose lost?"

"Eric's not here. He had to work. I- ah, bumped my face on a door. I wasn't looking where I was going."

"Are you sure?" Sadie looked at Dude with suspicion. "Did you do that, Dude? Jared didn't have that bruise last night."

Dude wouldn't look at her. He chomped out, "Nope," and kept eating like he hadn't been fed in a month.

Sisters. They always see more than you want them to. I had to sidetrack her.

"It's okay. I know Dude didn't do it. I'll take care of my nose and you take care of yours!" Then I felt bad for my smart mouth when Sadie looked at me sadly.

"I'm sorry, Sadie. I'll tell you more about it later, after I talk to Eric."

"You better. Or I will nark on you to Mom for being rude."

"Yeah, speaking of Mom, I miss her." I wasn't ashamed of it.

"Me, too," Sadie said with a big sigh. "I like being independent and running around with Becky, but I need a couple of Mom hugs."

"Hey, Beck, do you need a Mom hug?" Sadie asked when Becky came into the dining room carrying more food.

Becky looked up and smiled. "Yes! Are you people reading my mind? I was thinking that I should go home and get some clean clothes and see my parents." Then she saw our visitor and my nose. She pointed to him. "Dude? Did you and Jared get into it?"

"Nah. I'm feeding the poor guy. I'll tell you about it later."

When Dude finally looked up, he was actually smiling. "You are a great cook, Becky."

Becky looked embarrassed. "It was just bacon, eggs and toast."

"We've been living on granola bars and junk from the gas station."

"Doesn't Aunt Lulu feed you?"

"Nope. It's not part of the ...." Suddenly he looked like he had said too much. "Gotta go. Rub a dub-dub. Thanks for the grub," and he practically dove out the door.

"Wow. He moves fast," Becky said.

"Yeah, he must be half greyhound--or wolf." Sadie pointed to the empty plate. It looked like it had been licked clean.

CHAPTER TWENTY-FOUR

MMMMMAMA!

If you live in a bed and breakfast, work comes first. Just like at home. Clean first, then you can go. We scrubbed the kitchen and vacuumed the stairs. No one was checking in or out so we took towels to all the rooms, vacuumed, made the beds and straightened everything except Mr. Sneezy's room. No one had seen him for a couple of days. Come to think of it, I don't remember ever seeing him at all. It was as if he didn't exist, except for the sneezes which we all heard from time to time.

We were finished with our chores before lunch so Aunt Dodo told us to take the rest of the day off. She was feeling better so she was going to bake a cake and cookies, and work on a quilt.

"Yo, ladies! Let's go to the Island. We need to get together with Eric. I have a lot to tell him."

Sadie sighed, "But I want to see Mom first. I really miss Mom."

"Yeah, me, too. I also need clean clothes," Becky said.

It only took us an hour to get our backpacks filled with a few things for the day and hike down to the ferry.

"Eric is going to meet us with Apache and the buggy," Becky said.

"Good. I like buggy rides instead of walking." I was feeling a lot better, but sometimes my strength was about the same as a turtle with a semi- trailer attached.

"Yeah, that huge purple honker must weigh a lot. We'll let the horse drag it along for you." Sadie lightly punched my jaw and laughed when I yelled, "Ouch!" She reached out and touched my nose gently. "Sorry, Jared. I hope it's not broken. You don't even look like yourself. Maybe that's a good thing, hmm?"

"Sadie, you are asking for it!" But I could tell she was just teasing.

After a speedy ride to the island, we filed off the boat and hiked down the long ramp into town. Many strange things happened the last time we were on Mackinac Island. Some I would never like to repeat. I remembered how Sadie crashed her bike into Dr. Royalton while going down the same ramp we were walking on. He was the one who stopped in front of her and then rudely blamed her for the accident. If we had only known what we know now, I think I would have dumped him off the dock, right then and there. Down into the water with the pooping ducks.

But I like excitement, too and that summer was a lot of fun.

Eric took one skeptical look at my nose and said sarcastically, "Looks like you've got a story to tell us."

"Mmm hmmm. That I do.... Let's talk after we see Mom."

We were silent as Eric drove past the Hawk's Nest. I think we all wished we could go back to the way it was the last time we were together. I tried to be cool about it.

"Hey, guys? Who is sleeping in my bed this summer?" I was so jealous of whoever was staying in the loft I could almost feel myself turning green with envy.

"I'm not sure. Do you want to stop and see?" Eric grinned at Becky in a silly way. It made me a little suspicious.

"Uhh, sure. Do you think they'd care?"

"Nah. I'll bet they won't mind at all."

Becky opened the door and walked in. "I'm home, Mom!" she yelled.

"Your mom is here?" I asked. "Don't you still live next door in your grandpa's old home?"

A familiar voice came from the back room. "Becky and Eric! What are you doing here? E-E-E-E! Yippee! It's my kids." A short woman with blonde-streaked brown hair ran out and grabbed Sadie and me. It was great.

My mom was staying at the Hawk's Nest.

"Hey, Ma! We're home," I managed to squeak out before she squished both of us in a giant hug. I kept my sunglasses on and prayed she wouldn't notice my face for a while.

112

"I have been so lonesome without you both. When my cell phone quit, I felt lost. Your dad got me a new one and it just arrived in the mail today. I wish you could stay here, but I have to work open to close every day at the Gliding Wing. Joe and June Redhawk have to finish training two more people at the fudge store so June can run the Gliding Wing again. I wouldn't have anyone to feed you like Aunt Dodo does. So you would be on your own here, too."

"But Mom, if we stayed here we could come down and see you every day," Sadie begged.

"I'm sorry, Sadie, but I already paid Dodo for your food. I should be done here and back in St Ignace before the weekend. What is up with the dig and has anyone heard from Luke?"

"Mom, no one has heard from Luke," I stammered. "And Teya cancelled the wedding."

"Yes, Eric said she had. Wait and see. Things may change. Meanwhile, I have to keep working because I made a promise."

I was disappointed but I understood. Work always comes first in our family. It's the right thing to do, even if you have to clean twenty toilets a day. Yuck.

"All right…if you have to. We'll go back to St. Ignace without you." Then her eyes widened when she spotted my schnozz.

"Jared! What happened to your face?"

Uh oh, this isn't good. Now I gotta lie to my mom.

"I …uh… bumped it on a door. I kind of lost my balance and tripped over a rug…" *Lie-lie-lie-lie.*

"Wow. It looks like somebody smashed you in the face. Take off those glasses and let me look." Mom pulled me closer and I kind of melted into her and leaned my head on her shoulder. She smelled good. She felt my forehead for a temperature and carefully wiggled my nose and said, "You're very lucky. It's not broken. But you look pretty unrecognizable."

"Eh, who cares. I'm a big man, I'll deal with it."

Mom smacked me on the back. "I'm sure you will," she said. *That's where Sadie got those genes.*

"Here, let's put some tape on it. Maybe the poor nose will feel better." Mom spread a couple of layers of adhesive tape across my schnozz. It helped me breathe better.

That's all I need. A taped target for someone else to aim at. But I didn't dare take it off right then.

"Ma, can Becky and I work with you later today? It might be fun," Sadie begged.

"I remember how you moaned the last time about working for me. Are you sure?"

"Yeah, now that I know what real work is, I know your job is fun."

"Funny girl, I'll remind you of that statement when we're back home. Sure. I have a ton of pictures to mat and frame. You and Becky can do that like last time. I'll finish checking in the basket and jewelry orders. We got some beautiful new things in from Sam Whitepath, and a new artist, Angie Smith Massaway."

Eric gave me a sideways look and shrugged his head toward the door. "You guys want to see the new colt down at the corner barn? Dad might ship him and his mother to a farm up at Pickford before you guys come back over again so you better see him now."

"Sounds great. I'd love to see him," Sadie said.

"Yeah, sure. Okay.... I'm not crazy about big horses but I like small ones."

Once the gabbing started, it looked as if I'd be on my own later in the day, but that was okay. I was on the island. The Rock. Fudge Central and Horse Manure World.

A few minutes later, Mom took off on her bicycle and headed downtown to the Gliding Wing. We hopped into the buggy and Eric took us back to the stable.

Eric put his horse into a stall, pulled up some hay bales for us to sit on and got right to the point. "What's up, Fudge Breath?"

Confessing to everyone made me nervous. "As I passed Teya's tents yesterday I overheard someone threatening her. I didn't see who it was, but he was really nasty to her. I think she's being forced to do the dig. I went in to talk to her and she told me to mind my own business. So I gave her some advice and left."

"Advice?" Sadie asked.

"Stop the digging and ask for help."

"And she said she would?" Becky asked.

"No. I heard her crying when I left, so she must be really stressed."

"Teya cry? Couldn't be her. It must have been an evil spirit pretending to be her," Becky said.

"What else happened? Teya didn't do that to you, did she?" Eric pointed to my face.

"No." I waited until they were all looking at me. "A Wendigo did it last night."

Becky's eyes almost popped out of her head. "Ah- ah, Wendigo? Really?" Her voice sounded slightly choked up.

"Yep. It reached in the window, grabbed my shirt collar and yanked me forward into the window glass. I broke the glass with my forehead and smacked the window frame with my nose. He told me if I snooped around the tents anymore, he was going to eat me. Then he pushed me backwards onto the floor and left."

Becky jumped to her feet and paced back and forth. "I knew it! They *are* real!"

Eric yelled, "Come on Beck, they are not! Tell her, Fudge."

"He looked pretty real to me at the time, but I think it was makeup. Remember, I was half-asleep and didn't have my glasses on. It was mostly dark except for Teya's lights. The Wendigo tossed the window screen fifty feet from the house. When I went out and picked it up this morning, it had smudges of white makeup on the edge where he'd grabbed it. The window had a white handprint, too. I accused Dude, but he couldn't even say the word Wendigo. I fed him Becky's bacon and eggs and he promised to keep me informed about visitors to the site."

"Did you ask him why they moved the tents?"

"Nope. I forgot. The painful nose kind of took my mind off it."

Eric slapped his forehead. "Great. Makeup job or not, I'll have to sleep in Becky's room again for months. I can't be chasing her all over the island during her sleep-walking and nightmares."

Becky kind of laughed it off and said, "Oh I'm not that bad."

"Yes, you are," Sadie said. "Why do you think the desk was in front of the door this morning. Weren't you surprised to wake up with your ankle tied to the bed with a belt? You dream and then you run. I needed my sleep."

"Oh. Sorry." Becky didn't look sorry. She looked like she thought it was funny.

"See what I mean?" Eric said." I've been dealing with this all her life. Maybe Uncle Bushy has a big net at the hardware store that I can catch her with."

"Hey, I have an idea," Sadie said. "Take a big net and wrap the whole bottom bunk area with it. Then she'd be in her own cage and we'd all get some sleep."

Becky giggled, "Well, Sadie, you snore like a motor boat and talk in your sleep."

I pointed at Sadie. "Uh huh. I told you so. I'm not the only one who knows now. What did you dream about last night that made you run, Becky?"

Becky raised her arms up and waved them around. "The big marshmallow guy from the Ghost Buster's movie exploded and I was going to be buried in marshmallow. So I had to run away as fast as I could."

When we stopped laughing, we decided to glue my window screen in. Huron wouldn't be able to climb in anymore, but no one else could open it from the outside either.

After our planning session, Eric went back to work. We decided to meet at the new fudge store at five o'clock and go back to St. Ignace after dinner.

I walked the girls to the Gliding Wing and got ready to go for a short walk around the island.

"Jared, take my cell phone. Then we won't miss each other," Sadie said.

"Ahh, come on Sadie. It's pink and sparkly. I'll be back on time. I'm just going to spend the afternoon at the park or up at Eric's stable."

"I'm not chasing you down when I'm hungry."

"Okay. I'll take it with me, but I don't like phones—especially pink ones. I'll ignore all your BFF's calls. I feel like I'm on a string when I carry one." I gave Mom another hug. "Back in a while."

I slipped the cutesy phone into my pocket and turned to go out the door. I thought I saw someone familiar stroll past the window.

"Miss Ruffle?" Nah. Couldn't be.

CHAPTER TWENTY-FIVE

THE MISS RUFFLE SHUFFLE

There were probably two thousand tourists on the island. Could someone else in the whole world look like a human Shar-pei? Could someone else wear a blonde wig, a baggy flowered dress and drag a giant red bag that read, MR. PICKLE'S GOAT CHEESE? Yeah, they could. It would have to be someone from the very lonely city of Repulsiveville— not anybody who was normal.

I knew Sadie wouldn't believe me, but I was going to try. "Sadie, I think I saw Miss Ruffle outside the window."

Sadie was hanging a new picture on the display wall behind the counter. She had no view of the street, but snorted and said, "Ha. That is not a funny joke, Jared. She's too old and crazy to come all the way up here by herself."

"It sure looks like her. Tell Mom I am going to follow her and see."

"Go for it. You don't have anything better to do until five o'clock anyway. Stalking an old lady might be fun." Sadie went into the back room to tell Becky and Mom and the laughing sounded like a pond full of loons.

I followed the strange old woman who looked like Miss Ruffle. I sure hoped nobody thought I was stalking her. Ugh, the idea gave me the creeps.

She stared in the window of the Antique Geek next door to us for a couple of minutes. I hurried into the store across the street before she saw me in the window reflection. I don't know how, but the clerk recognized me from my last trip to the island. She pointed to the door. "OUT! This is not a fudge store!"

I left quickly. But it's nice to know my professional fudge tasting reputation is still intact on the island.

I noticed Miss Ruffle's shuffling walk. It seemed familiar to me, but it could have been because she was wearing curly-toed green slippers with bells on the toes. Her next stop was another expensive jewelry store, and this time she went in.

I ducked into a kid's clothes and toy store. No problems there from the staff. I peeked out the front window and watched her leave. A few minutes later she stopped, looked at her watch, and almost ran down Market Street to the ferry. Her big blonde wig flopped back and forth on her head like a mop. Half the time it covered her face, and I was sure she was going to lose it or step in something horse-flavored at any second.

I decided I'd call Eric and let him come and see Miss Ruffle for himself.

"Yo, horsy man, I'm down at the west dock. You gotta come see Miss Ruffle. Uh huh, I'm positive it's her."

He rode up on a rusty bike that looked as if it was ready to fall apart.

"Where did you get that thing?"

"Grandpa. It's so old nobody's gonna steal it. I oil it up and keep the tires inflated. It goes great downhill. There are no uphill gears, but I need to work out anyway."

"It's almost as ugly as that." I pointed at Miss Ruffle standing alone on the dock. She looked very strange and people nearby were giving her lots of space.

"Yowsers! I thought when you said she looked like a Shar-pei you meant she was dog ugly. But she really does look like a Shar-pei. Except for that nose...."

"Let's follow her," I said. "Then we'll know what she's up to."

"Nah, I gotta work. Here, take my passbook so you can come back over for dinner. My dad's paying for the meal and I'm gonna chow down big time."

The ferry was pulling up to the docks and Miss Ruffle was first in line for St. Ignace. She never looked back at me so I decided it was now or never.

"See ya later. I better call Sadie and tell her."

I called Mom's phone and Sadie answered.

"Sadie! It *is* Miss Ruffle. She's getting on the boat to St. Ignace and I'm going to follow her back."

There was a lot of squawking going on in the background for a minute and my mom grabbed the phone.

"Jared, please be careful. You know she's not very nice. Your dad suspects she might be the prankster. She drove away right after we did and nothing has happened at our house since then."

"I'm just going to follow her. I'm staying as far away from her as I can."

"Good. Make sure she doesn't recognize you. Do you have money for a ticket to come back for dinner?"

"Eric lent me his commuter ticket book. Gotta run. She's getting on the boat. I'll be careful and be back by five for dinner. See you later."

It was time to spy.

Even though it was hot out, I raised my sweatshirt hood, and stuck on my sunglasses. With my taped fat purplish nose and bruised forehead, she would never recognize me. I followed behind fifty people and at least fifty more followed behind me. At the top of the ramp, a member of the ferry crew gave me a second look. "Ouch! Nice nose, man," he said, and took a ticket from Eric's commuter ticket book. As I walked aboard, I glanced down the steps and scanned the ferry's lower deck. Miss Ruffle's wild wig wasn't down there. She must be hot from her run down to the ferry. I looked up top and there she was, right at the front of the boat. I hopped into the furthest back seat next to somebody's grandma, tightened my hood and prepared to blast off.

After all the usual announcements, the boat backed out and took off. As we zoomed out of the harbor and passed the lighthouses, the wind raked through all the people on the upper deck. It blew hair, hats and clothing everywhere. I didn't have time to admire the view as the Grand Hotel floated past. I was watching Miss Ruffle. Her big hairy hand clenched the floppy wig onto her head, but the wind lifted it up enough for me to see a manly wrinkled neck, short black hair, and a big bald spot under the wig.

CHAPTER TWENTY-SIX

SPY TIME

I hurried off the boat as fast as I could and stood next to a van, trying to look as if I was waiting to get in. I pulled my hood as tight to my face as I could and kept the dark glasses on. When I heard Miss Ruffle's jingling slippers and heavy panting, I turned away so she couldn't see my face.

She crossed the parking lot and went into a little mall by the dock. I casually followed her into the mall and saw her go into the family restroom. I strolled over to the tee shirt store, looked through twenty tee shirts, and tried to watch the restroom door at the same time.

"Hey, you! Kid in the hoodie! You buying or stealing?" a grumpy old man with, 'I AIN'T NO SAINT' on his tee shirt, shouted at me. I agree with the shirt.

"Huh? Ahh… buying, I guess."

"Well, hurry it up, I'm closing early today. Ten percent off if you buy a purple one."

A purple one that said, 'BEWARE OF PEOPLE WHO DISLIKE CATS.' Hmm is that a hint or something? Maybe he thinks it matches my nose.

"Sold! Do you have it in an extra large?" I looked back at the rest room door and it stood wide open.

Miss Ruffle was gone.

I bought the shirt and ran out the door. Around the corner of the building, I crashed into a man and stepped all over his feet.

"Oops, sorry, mister." The man looked like Buffalo Bill. He wore a western shirt, jeans, cowboy hat, and a gray handlebar mustache half the size of the Mackinac Bridge.

"That's okay, son." His voice was low and gravelly. "You walk on the tops of my feet and I'll walk on the bottoms." I had stomped on his fancy cowboy boots. He carried a thick briefcase and he was munching pork rinds.

I checked my watch and saw that it was 4:30. I had accomplished nothing. Miss Ruffle had disappeared, and the sight of the pork rinds had made me hungry. I thought about going to the inn for a snack and headed that direction.

A horn honked and I looked up. I saw Mr. Mustache meet a man who climbed out of a white van and together they walked toward the Museum of Ojibwa Culture. As they entered the door, "Wa-choo!" Mr Mustache sneezed so hard his hat tipped forward and covered his face. The back of his head looked like

Miss Ruffle's head. I almost yelled, "It's him! Her! Miss Ruffle! Whoever. Now what do I do?"

Sadie's newest favorite song blasted out of the sparkly pink phone. I grabbed it and hoped no one near me noticed the color.

"What?" I felt like Dad answering his phone.

"If you're still in St. Ignace, get back here!" Sadie said. "We're going to a cool place for supper and you get to test some new gourmet fudge." *Oh, sweet fudge angel, I adore you!*

"Okay. Sounds good to me." I tried to remain calm as I delivered my news. "I've got a lot to tell everybody later, but I can't wait. Miss Ruffle is a man!"

"Mom! Mom!" Sadie screeched. "Jared says Miss Ruffle *is* a man!"

CHAPTER TWENTY-SEVEN

FORT DE BUADE MUSEUM

When I woke up the next day after stuffing myself on prime rib at the Steak Town Grille, I felt great. It must have been all that protein. I almost felt human again.

Eric was still on Mackinac Island, slinging fudge. I will admit that even if the bacon caramel chocolate fudge was magnificent, too much of a good thing can kill you. But wow, what a wonderful way to go.

Aunt Dodo let Sadie, Becky, and me go for a walk after breakfast clean up. We wanted to look around St. Ignace a little. I stuffed Sadie's camera, a few snacks and some bottles of water into a backpack and hiked out the door.

"Gee, dorky bro, why all the provisions? Are you hungry already?"

"I'd rather be safe than sorry, Sadie. You never know what's going to happen when you go out walking."

"Yeah, Fudge Breath," Becky said. "Since we have to be back by 11:00 to help with check-outs and rooms, where do you want to go in such a short time?"

"Hmm. I don't know." I looked behind Becky and down the street. Something had changed since yesterday. "When did that trailer in the Little Bear lot show up? It looks like nobody is using it." The trailer had a flat tire and the door faced some bushes. It almost blended into the greenery. It didn't look like it was going anywhere for a while.

We went over by the white carnival-type trailer. " FIERO'S FIERY CHILI DOGS AND TACOS. Look, fry bread is on the menu, too. That's different, maybe a Native American runs it."

"That's odd," Sadie said. "They're not planning to sell anything because the windows are covered with paper on the inside. Most of the food trailers are further down town. I don't see anyone else around here."

"Maybe someone's using it for storage," Sadie said. "There are already a hundred food stands around here."

"Mmm, chili dogs and tacos." My stomach growled. "I know, let's go to the Fort De Buade museum for a while. But first, let's go to Bentley's and have a chili dog and fries."

Becky whapped me on the shoulder and said, "Hey dork, we ate a huge breakfast. Get going."

"Okay. Okay." I rubbed my shoulder. "You're spending way too much time with Sadie. It's rubbing off."

We fought our way through the crowds of car people and finally arrived at the museum entrance. I was surprised to see someone who looked very familiar walking into the museum. Someone I did not like.

Sadie and Becky were busy laughing at a red truck spinning its tires in the middle of the street and never noticed the visitor. "Whoo-hoo! Look at him burn up those tires." Becky yelled.

The wind off the lake blew the burned rubber smoke at us until we choked.

Sadie yelled at the truck. "Grow up, loser. You're making air pollution. Cough, cough."

"Never mind," Becky said. "That dorky driver is somebody's grandpa. He must be at least ninety."

"Psst. Quiet! Teya went in ahead of us," I said.

"She did? Wonder why she's in there?" Sadie rubbed the smoke out of her eyes.

I looked at her and said, "I don't know. She says she *is* an archaeologist ….and it is a free country, so I guess she can go anywhere she wants."

Becky made a face. "Why do you think she's here, Sadie? I think she's probably planning to steal something."

"Yeah, she has light fingers, a rotten attitude, and she's likely to steal important stuff right before your eyes," Sadie agreed with Becky. "And if she's a vampire she can hypnotize people, and no one will see her. Oh, Oh! Maybe *she* was the Wendigo!"

"Teya, the vampire, hypnotizes people? Teya, the Wendigo? Nope. That was a man who jerked me around. He was too tall and strong to be skinny Teya. "

I couldn't believe what I was hearing. Both the girls had crashed off the deep end.

"She didn't vampno-tize me. I am still very sensible," Becky said.

"I'm not so sure about that statement, Becky, but we'll watch her. You two go in like you always do, say 'hi' to everybody and pretend you don't know she's in there. Go to the bathroom or something, then go around to the far end of the building and come back toward her. I will follow a few yards behind her."

"Whaa-choo!" a sneeze resounded through the open door of the museum. Hmm, that sneeze sounded familiar. I peeked in.

I could hardly believe my eyes. Two people I never expected to see together. It was Mr. Mustache talking to Teya.

I grabbed the girls and pulled them back out of sight. "Shh-shh! Don't let them see you." I pointed into the museum.

Becky peeked around the corner, and then Sadie.

"So, she's talking to an old man wearing a cowboy hat. What's so important about that?" Becky asked.

"It's Miss Ruffle in disguise. That's the guy who sneezed and when his cowboy hat tipped forward I saw his bald head."

"What? I don't understand. Your brain is off track, bro."

"Arrgh! Sadie will you listen to me?" Nothing was coming out of my mouth right.

130

As calm as I could I said, "That's the guy I saw morph from Miss Ruffle," I pointed.

"I understand. He is a she, who morphed into a he," Becky said. "I get it. It's *that* guy... ha-ha-ha!"

"Oh, never mind. You two inhaled too much burned rubber smoke. Those two should not know each other and if they do, we have a real problem on our hands. St Ignace may never recover from whatever they have planned."

CHAPTER TWENTY-EIGHT

EAVESDROPPER

"Okay, follow the plan. Go in like I told you and keep watch. Pretend you don't see them. I'll follow and listen to what they're saying."

Becky said, "Gee, Jared. Any more orders for us poor little women?"

I rolled my eyes and sighed, "Just do it."

A neat dugout that had once been buried in the sand on the lakeshore sat on a table near the door. There were many other interesting exhibits, too, but Teya was moving fast and I had snooping to do.

I stopped and pretended to read one of the exhibit cards so I could hear what Mr. Mustache was saying. "Listen, Teya. You aren't getting out of this….leave a door open … your da… the Frenchman is dangerous. He wants whatever you find… medicine bags…bones. I'll get the one here in the back room case …keep the kids guessing and busy… Be watching you…"

The scratchy scary voice faded away. It gave me the creeps like fingernails on a chalkboard.

Slinking a little closer I hid behind a wall of Civil War items.

I heard Teya ask, "Why are you helping him if he's so dangerous?"

"He'll be more dangerous if he doesn't get what he wants."

"I thought there was no honor among thieves," she sneered. "He means nothing to me and he disgusts me."

"He helped me get out of prison so I owe him."

"Your Da...the Frenchman... wants the bags, so do it or else."

"No! If he wants more, he has to pay me more money, and I want it now. I don't like doing this. It's disgusting."

"Dr. Dove, is this man bothering you?" A large man carrying a long wooden baggataway stick strode up. I saw Sadie and Becky hiding behind a case of dolls in the background.

"Why, yes, he is annoying me. Please make him leave."

The man in the mustache touched his hat and nodded to the large man. "Sorry, sir, I'll be going." As he passed Teya, he shot an angry look at her and snarled, "Remember what I said, young lady," but she ignored him.

CHAPTER TWENTY-NINE

LOONY WOMAN AND MR. MUSTACHE

I ducked down behind the wall as the big man escorted Mr. Mustache out. I didn't want him to know I was in there.

Sadie and Becky strode up to Teya and Sadie said, "Hey, Teya, did we rescue you from that creep or what?"

"What made you think I wanted to be rescued?" Teya spat back at Sadie.

Sadie jerked back. "We thought he was going to hurt you, so we sent Mr. Riley over to help you."

"You thought wrong, little girls. What I do is none of your business. I can take care of myself." Teya stuck her nose in the air and walked away with her queen attitude on.

Becky's face got very red. She stalked after Teya and shouted, "You big phony. You are a big **Mahwee Binoojiing!**"

Sadie ran over and put her hand over Becky's mouth. "Shh! Don't say something you might get arrested for."

Becky pulled Sadie's hand away and grinned. "What? I called her a crying baby."

"That's all? It sure sounded like something bad. Tell me the word for loon?"

"**Mahng**," Becky said.

"Yep, that's her, the looooony woman," Sadie said wiggling her fingers as if she was putting a spell on Teya. "Oooh! Come on and vampno-tize me, you crazy loony woman.

"That would be **Mahng gikway**. **Kway** means woman. Let's go," Becky said. "I'm going to the other museum to talk to some people from the tribe right now. I have had enough of her." Sadie walked past Teya saying, "Mahng, Mahng, Mahng." Teya ignored her and walked into another area.

I stayed where I was. Mr. Mustache left the building too easily. He was so persistent he might come back into the museum disguised as Miss Ruffle. But why anyone would want to look like her unless they were forced to at gunpoint?

I stayed in the room with the Native American objects. I was trying to figure out what was going on when Teya returned to the room. I stood behind a tall case, pulled out the camera, shut off the flash and waited. She unlocked and opened the back door a crack, "Click." *Nice pose for your mug shot, Teya.* She left the room quickly and in came Mr. Mustache. He was in such a hurry he didn't even bother to wait until the museum closed.

I waited until he was almost inside and, "Click." I got a picture of him coming in.

He turned his head my way and I ducked behind a wall. I crept back down the hallway to the lobby. I didn't want to let him know it was me who found him.

"Mr. Riley. The man you told to leave the museum just snuck in through an open back door."

"Oh yeah? I'll go take care of him!" I sat on the bench in front of the museum to wait and see how soon Mr. Riley would toss Mr. Mustache out on his mustache.

Five minutes later, Mr. Mustache dashed from the museum with Mr. Riley following close behind swinging the baggattaway stick. I turned away and covered my face with my hand so he couldn't recognize me.

"…and if you come back, I'll use this thing on you first and then I'll call the police," Mr. Riley yelled. He waved the baggataway stick in the air to intimidate the man in the moustache. Mr. Mustache muttered curses as he jogged past me and headed north. I pushed my way through the crowd and went south looking for Bentley's Restaurant, and a chilidog and fries.

Yes, I am a squealer, a snitch, and a nark, but if I can stop one more thing from being stolen, I will yell all I can.

CHAPTER THIRTY

THE BONEY COLLECTOR'S COLLECTION

I never found Sadie and Becky while I was at Bentley's and when I left, I was reeking of chilidogs and onions. I had a couple more hours before I had to be back at the Inn, so I went in search of the Boney Collector and its owner.

I strolled up to the dig where Dude was sitting in a lawn chair in the shadow of his tent. I gave him a regulation salute. "Dude! How's it going?"

Dude grabbed his forehead like he had a headache, heaved a big sigh and said, "What do you want now? Haven't you bugged me enough?"

"*I* have bugged *you*? Nay, my good man, I have only fed you. Or did you forget?" I put on my highly offended face. "I have bugged your sister because she acts so guilty. You on the other hand don't behave in the same suspicious manner."

"Cut the crap, Jared. I know you want something." *How did he know me so well?*

"Okay. I do want something. I want to see the inside of your cool car. The way it's made is driving me crazy."

Dude laughed, "Ha. Is that all you want? You must have some other hidden reason." He went to a cooler, took out a bottle of red stuff and chugged it. He made a face afterward. "Gack! Do you want some vitamins and energy drink? I mix it up with tomato juice to try to make it taste better!"

So much for Becky's idea that he was slurping down a bottle of blood. "No thanks. Keep your vitamins. I just want an explanation of why your hearse is built with the crack down the top and the split back doors."

"It's my DJ table and platform. My stepfather owns a body shop and we built it together." He pulled out his keys. "Watch."

He opened the car door and took out a big tire iron. He unlocked the rear hatch door and used the end of the iron to take out some bolts. The sides dropped down and the back end of the car opened like a big clamshell. Dude reached inside and flipped out some speakers and the coffin was exposed.

I was amazed. He was showing me *the coffin*. Dude stepped onto the trailer hitch and leaped into the back. Then he reached into the coffin and took out a remote control. He pushed a button and with a loud grinding noise, the coffin raised up about three feet. It was so cool.

138

"I've got a mega set of batteries to run this thing, but I need to plug it in for a while. Can you run this cord over to the outdoor plug on the front porch?"

"Sure." I took the 20-foot orange cord to the La Croix's house and plugged it in.

Dude stepped up into the back of the hearse, leaned over the coffin and opened it all the way until the top lay flat. Then he hooked a skull on the front of the DJ table, put some earphones and a mike on, pushed a few buttons and adjusted a few slides on the dash. I jumped when the screaming sounds of heavy metal rock blasted into the air. A loud shout of: "I am the Boney Collector! I dig up music from the ancient past to the slammin' jammin' present!" came from Dude.

That explained the CDs and the unusual dash on the car. It explained everything. What a cool set up.

"All right!" I heard someone yell from the street behind us and people from the car show started walking toward us.

"Looks like you're going to be putting on a show right now."

"Great." Dude adjusted his dark glasses and squinted at the growing crowd. "I didn't mean to have it so loud. The dance is tonight over at Little Bear's parking lot. This will be great advertising."

"So that's your new job?" I asked.

Dude held a CD close to his face to read the label. "I'll still finish the painting for Aunt Dodo, but this pays much better. A grand for three hours of work will keep me in vitamins for a couple of months."

When he shoved his dark glasses up onto his forehead and yanked out a magnifying glass to check his list of music, I saw his strange white eyes again.

"Oh yeah, I can't forget the tip jar." He brought out a big clear jar with skulls painted on it. A single dollar bill was lying loosely inside.

"This jar is magic," he said. "People fill it up and I empty it into my pocket. Cha-ching!"

People were coming closer and shouting out their favorite songs. It reminded me of the scary scene in the Frankenstein movie where the crowd chases down the monster. The only thing missing were the flaming torches.

"Well, I guess I'll go. Looks like you're going to be busy for a while."

He looked embarrassed when he said, "Wait, Jared, I can't see very well. Teya usually pulls the CDs for me but she's busy. Since this was your idea, can you stay and help out?"

"No problem, Dude, I dig great music."

"Cool!" He pulled his dark glasses back down and announced, "Ladies and gents, the party is at 7 tonight over in Little Bear's parking lot. But I'll be glad to play whatever you want for one hour!"

I looked back at the tents. Teya stepped out of the little tent and stared at us. Then I thought I saw her smile.

Suddenly the whole world shook from an enormous explosion. Dude and I both jumped skyward.

140

CHAPTER THIRTY-ONE

FIGURING STUFF OUT

My heart jumped into my throat. Either that or I swallowed several frogs...with hip boots on.

Dude shuddered, shook off the noise and said, "Hey man, I think they're getting ready to shoot off some fireworks."

"Yeah, or blow something up." I couldn't get excited about loud noises anymore. Not since a smelly voyageur tried to massage my body with a shotgun blast.

We played rock and heavy metal requests for an hour and a half, but we couldn't get people to leave. Finally, Dude and turned off the music and announced, "Remember, the dance is at seven o'clock in the Little Bear Arena parking lot! See you there." Amidst the groans of the disappointed crowd, he closed the coffin and climbed down. I helped him close the sides.

"I've got to go to work now, but I'll get the rest of the gang to come over to help you with the show tonight. About six thirty, okay? No charge, man. It should be a gas."

"Cool. See ya later." Dude flicked his hat sideways in a salute and went back to arranging his moldy oldie CD's and taking early requests from the lingering crowd.

Heading back to the Inn, I met Teya hiding as usual under her black hat.

"**Chinodin**... I mean, Jared. Why are you helping my brother?"

"Dude's a cool guy. We're going to help him out tonight, too. You going to the dance?"

Teya shook her head, "No. I have an appointment Thomas doesn't know about." She lifted her nose and brought out her queen attitude. "And don't ask me with who or what it's about because I'm not explaining anything else."

She turned and stalked into the little tent.

"Still the bad girl," I mumbled to myself. "Appointment, huh? Maybe I should check out that appointment."

Eric occupied the porch swing. He was flat out on the short seat, one foot up tangled in the chain, and the other foot dragging on the floor. The rusty old swing swayed hypnotically back and forth slowly.

"'Cha doing, Fudge Breath?" Creak, creak, squee-eek.

"Figuring stuff out, Ponytail."

"Cool music. Finally saw the inside of the coffin?" Creak, creak, squee-eek.

I dropped into a chair. "Yep. It's a disc jockey sound board and speakers. The coolest setup you ever saw."

"Hmm. Takes a lot of money for a get-up like that. Wonder where it came from?" He swayed some more on the swing and yawned. He made me sleepy as I watched him.

"He says his step-dad owns a body shop. He helped him make it." I yawned, "Doing anything tonight? I told Dude we'd all help him with the music. Teya told me she's not helping him because she has an appointment that Dude doesn't know about. She's not giving up yet."

"Hmm, appointment? You should check that out, Fudge. I'll be over there. Nappin' now. Talk later…after caffeine. Sno-rrr." Eric drifted off.

I guess I won't have the swing until a lot later. Before Eric had me asleep on my feet, I headed off to find the girls and fill them in on their jobs for tonight.

As I left Eric, another explosion blasted through the sky. I looked back to see Eric sitting straight up in the swing, shaking his fist at the bay where the fireworks barge floated. "Would ya shut up for a while? Ya idiots!"

CHAPTER THIRTY-TWO

DUDE! YOU'RE A ROCKSTAR

"**D**ance! Dance! Dance! All ya wanna do is dance, dance, dance!" the music shouted at the crowd. And that was all they wanted to do.

I never saw so many golden oldies. And I'm not talking about music. Those car people were same age as my grandparents and they acted younger than I did. They were doing the Twist, the Swim, and the Hitchhiker, but the strangest one was the Watusi. They danced to War, Night Fever, Joy, YMCA, Bullfrogs, Bad Girls, the Beatles, Temptations and a whole lot of names that I found in the file but had never heard before. I saw Eric's three aunts dancing in a corner of the lot to a song my mom mumbled occasionally, "Don't Stop Believing."

There were people coming from everywhere. Someone had set lights up for the dance and it was almost as bright as an NFL stadium during a night game.

Dude wore his hooded red suit with a glow-in-the-dark skeleton painted on the front of it. The back of his black cape read 'THE BONEY COLLECTOR' in sparkling sequins. He was wild. He danced around like a crazy man while the music played. If we hadn't been having so much fun, I would have teased him about his goofy outfit.

About an hour and half into the dance, we took Dude with us on a break. Aunt Dodo made us a pile of sub sandwiches and we ate on the front porch.

Dude plopped onto the porch, sucked on a bottle of cola and sighed, "Bushed and beat." He looked out at Lake Huron and asked, "Why is this place called Mackinac?"

Becky stared at him as if he was from outer space. "Why do you want to know?"

"It's an interesting place. The island and the bridge are Mackina*c* with a C, but the city on the other side of the bridge is Mackina*w*, with a W. Why isn't it the same?"

"Mackina*c* with an C is French," Becky said. "Mackina*w*, with a W is English. They both sound the same. It all started with the Anishinabe word **Mish-nni-maki-nong**. **Mish** means great, **nni** is a connecting sound, **maki** means a crevice or crack, and **nong** means land or place."

"Oh," Sadie said, "do you mean like the crack in the ground on Mackinac Island? The one Eric said a spirit lived in and I'd step on his fingers if I was too close?"

"Same one," Becky said. "So Mackinac means 'the land of the big crevice.' There's the one on the island

and one here on the mainland. It's behind us and a little south. Warm air used to come out of it all winter so people stayed near it. Scientists think that this crevice was connected to the one on the island. When they put in the city's sewer system part of it was filled in."

"You're kidding," Dude said.

"Nope. Completely true."

Becky pointed at the old church building down the hill near where Teya kept moving the tents. "Mr. Riley said this whole area had a lot of activity in the late 1600's and early 1700's. Right where your tents are was the mission of St. Ignace. The Ottawa, Chippewa and Huron tribes surrounded the mission. Fort De Buade was south of here a little.

The priests at the mission hated the soldiers because they influenced the native people in bad ways. The Fort's commander, Cadillac, was so angry with the priests, he moved everyone to Detroit to get away from the priests. Not long afterward an old priest burned the mission down and went to Quebec because no one was here for him to teach."

"Now buildings, roads, and the old railroad track have covered the fort and mission up. Everything is gone except the Anishinabe people. They came back to St. Ignace from Detroit and aren't going anywhere."

"Does anybody know where the old fort is?" Dude asked in a sleepy voice.

"No, not really," Becky said. "Everybody has ideas about where it could be, but since sometime before 1755 it was moved to Mackinaw City and renamed Fort

Michilimackinac, it's going to be hard to find. But they found Fort St. Joseph down in Niles so they'll find this one someday."

"Hey guys, did you know that Teya and I are Keepers of the Fire." Dude's lazy voice stopped us all. "On my mother's side, that is."

"Really?" Becky's mouth flew open. "**Odaywatomi?** Potawatomi? Then why are you so pale? Ouch! Don't hit me, Sadie."

"There are a lot of pale-faced Native Americans in my family. Genes are strange." He got very quiet and I thought he went to sleep. Then he said, "Teya and I are albinos."

For once Becky couldn't say anything. Finally, she said, "I am so sorry, Dude. I thought you and Teya were something else..."

"I know... vampires. I like to play games with people and pretend I am one. It's easier and a whole lot more interesting than explaining the truth. Teya doesn't like me to scare people. She tries to pretend she's normal. That's why she colors her hair and wears brown contacts."

I looked at him in the porch light. He was so light he seemed to glow a little. "Are you kidding me, Dude? You're normal. So you're extra pale— the whole world is made of different colors. That's what makes it interesting."

Becky reached out and gently tapped Dude on the shoulder. "I really am sorry. Will you forgive me?"

"Yeah. Sure. You weren't as mean to us as a lot of people have been. And you fed me, too." He grinned. "It was good."

I heard a thump and looked around. "Hey people, look over there. Somebody's moving around in the trees near the trailer." Then I didn't see them anymore. "Did you see anyone go into the trailer?"

Dude rolled to his side and looked at the trailer, "Nah," and lay back down.

"Where?" Eric said. "All I see is that huge crowd waiting by the Boney Collector. Dude, you are a rock-star, man! Whew-hoo!" He whistled. "Go, Dude, go!"

"Thanks, man, appreciate it. Need the dough... maybe I'll get another gig..." his voice trailed off.

"How much cola did you have tonight, Eric?" Becky asked.

"Enough to keep me going for the whole night!" He drummed on the porch rail. "Hey, Dude, you famous DJ rock-star, let's go back and get busy! The fireworks start soon and this car show will be over for the night."

"Dude? Dude? Wake up, Dude. It's your time to shine." I shook him and he snored. "Uh...guys, I think Dude is really out. I guess caffeine doesn't bother him."

CHAPTER THIRTY-THREE

THE OSHKIBIMADIZEEG—
THE NEW PEOPLE ARRIVE

After we woke Dude up and fed him some more cola, he finished the dance and we headed back to the Inn. I was glad I finally understood why Dude and Teya wore strange clothing and acted in such strange ways. Sun is very unhealthy for vampires—and albinos.

I grabbed another history book off the shelf and went back to my room to read. My paper was just about finished. Every day I spent in St. Ignace gave me new ideas on how to finish it. Life in the 1600's and 1700's was difficult for everyone, no matter who you were or where you lived. If you didn't catch something like black plague or die of a disease or infection, somebody might shoot an arrow through you just because they didn't like your face.

Somewhere in the distance, I heard music. I couldn't place the song. It might have been because my ears were still ringing from three hours of Dude's loud music, but it sounded like some kind of wail. The sound was sad, but somewhat excited all at the same time. I went to the window and saw a crowd of people by the glowing tents. Drums pounded and people swayed back and forth with the echoing beat.

I ran downhill and when I got to the crowd, someone was speaking.

"Our families have lived here for thousands of years. Taking the dead back from Mother Earth will upset the harmony and balance of our land. Return the bones of the ancients to the ground. Too many people have dug here for too many years. The bones are crying out. It's time to let the **Chiahyaog,** our elders, rest.

"All the earth belongs to the **Gitchie Manito**, the Great Spirit," the speaker said. "We only borrow it for a time. We are here to heal the land."

"Go away!" Teya shouted. "This is not your business!" and returned to the tent.

I decided to snoop again. I went to the back of the tent and listened. I was always nosy for a good cause.

"It's okay to stop digging, sis," Dude said.

"I finally found what the Frenchman wants and he will be coming back to get it. Get away from here, while you can, Thomas. Here! Take this money. Go up to Partridge's Bed and Breakfast. You'll be safe up there."

"But I don't want to leave you behind with these people," Dude yelled. "I know I can protect you!"

"Our real father is here and he's threatening to take you away if I don't finish digging. I only have one more area to check and I'll be done."

"He can't do that. You are my guardian."

"Yes, he can. You aren't eighteen yet, Thomas Dove Marquette. Go! Get out of here! I will take care of this."

"I'm not leaving."

"You don't understand. He will hurt you."

"If he is the man who told me to move the tents and then slapped me, I'm not going with him."

"Yes. He wants me to find proof that we are related to Jacques Marquette so he can inherit some property in Laon, France. I am digging up every scrap of bone I can find for him. Now, escape while you can."

"Hmm. Now I understand," I mumbled. I jumped when someone tapped me on the shoulder.

"Psst. Fudge Breath. Why are you back here? Let's go!" Eric hissed. "We don't want to be caught in this mess."

"Who are these people? Are they going to hurt Teya and Dude?"

"Who knows? Go up to Aunt Dodo's now. We don't know what their plans are."

Eric and I walked back up to Aunt Dodo's Inn.

"Mrow?" Huron grabbed onto my pant leg. I picked him up, and without a nose tickle or an itch, carried him back to the porch.

WE were met on the porch by fuzzy white Nagamoon who let out with a low sad cry, "Mee-eee-rowl-rowl-rowl". Both cats sat and watched with us as smoke from burning smudge pots filled the air. The sad song and cries from the crowd raised the hair on my neck.

What I overheard Teya say to Dude finally sunk into my brain. "Eric, we have to stop this. It's all about bones. Marquette's bones." When Eric's mouth opened, I said, "Trust me."

Eric and I headed back down and saw Becky standing at the back of the crowd. Her head jerked toward me and her frown almost sent me back up hill with one stare.

"Wait, Beck. Stop the protest. We have to take the time to figure this out. It's too complicated to explain now. I overheard a man threaten Teya and Dude. I recognized his voice."

Becky's angry face changed to a suspicious glare. "What did you hear?"

I whispered, "Remember what you told Sadie and me about bones? Old bones? I heard that the Frenchman wants old medicine bags. This may even be about Father Marquette's bones.... I need more proof myself."

Becky thought for a second and then she raced over to the drummers and the pounding stopped.

"**Chinodin** has something to say." She folded her arms and looked at the crowd with an upset look on her face.

I felt a big wave of disapproval as the whole group turned to stare at me. Did everyone in town know me as **Chinodin**? I decided to stop talking so much.

"I guarantee things will end soon and the bones of the elders won't cry anymore. Please be patient."

Someone in the crowd yelled, "What do you know! No! We won't stand for the desecration any more!" And the crowd rushed forward. A tall man unzipped the door of the large tent— no one was inside. He ran to each tent and opened the flaps.

Dude and Teya were gone. They had escaped the angry crowd.

The people became so quiet, I heard the night birds talking to each other.

Before anyone spoke, I turned and went back up the hill. I didn't wait around to see what would happen next.

Half way up the hill, I spotted a familiar looking man in dark clothes hiding behind a tree, watching the crowd. I couldn't place him in my mind. When he saw me staring at him, he stepped back into the brush and he also disappeared.

CHAPTER THIRTY-FOUR

COWBOY BOOTS

"Ow. Ow. Ouch! Will you stop rubbing my sore head?" I opened my eyes to see the whole family looking at me. "What happened now?"

"Jared, are you okay?" I looked up Aunt Dodo's nose. *Oooh, Hairy!*

"My head hurts." I reached up and felt a huge lump and a cut. "Ow! How did I get out here in the living room?" Sadie and Becky were crying over in the corner. "What's wrong?"

"We woke up when we heard you shouting 'Fire! Fire!' and came down and found the smudge pot was on fire and you were lying on the ground and all Grandpa's stuff is gone!" Becky bawled. "Somebody took all his powwow things."

"What? No way!" I sat up. "Ow...head...dizzy." I had to hold my head in my hands to keep it from falling off. "Who did it?" The broken smudge pot lay on its side on the floor with still warm ashes strewn around. A trail of big footprints and little kitty footprints tracked through the soot and ashes and spread it all over the room and out the door. It looked like something was dragged through those tracks, too.

"Are you sure you don't know?" Becky pointed at my hands. "You have black smudges all over."

"Mrow?" Huron popped out from under the sofa. His gray fur was splotched with black ashes.

"Uh oh." Sadie wiped her eyes as she picked up Huron. "Was this fuzzy boy your assistant." Huron leaped out of her arms, leaving dirty paw prints on her back and arms, and walked over and sat on my stomach. "Well, now we know how you got your smudge marks. Huron did it all."

"Huron! That's it! I remember Huron waking me up and wanting to go out. I walked into the living room and saw the smudge pot flaming. I started yelling and then the last thing I remember is ...cowboy boots?" *Where have I seen cowboy boots before?*

Aunt Dodo had a funny look on her face. "Did you say cowboy boots? We had a guest... but he left this afternoon."

"Did he have a cowboy hat and a huge gray moustache that sticks out like wings on his face? He kind of twirls it."

"Oh, the guy from the museum," Sadie gasped. "Again?"

Aunt Dodo started the computer and read the register. "No. That wasn't him. This guest's name was Roberto Fiero. He has a Michigan driver's license, and an odd car license number, SMINE2. He's short, wears a baseball cap, big sunglasses, Hawaiian shirt and cut off jeans. He had a gray ponytail sticking out through the back of the cap. It seemed strange to wear those clothes with cowboy boots. I don't think he ever changed his clothes all the time he was here. He wore the same wild shirt checking in and out. I don't think I ever saw him leave his room. Ugh. I hope he took a bath sometime while he was here."

"Oh," Beck said, "I remember him from when he checked in. He was weird."

"Why didn't I ever see this guy? I'm here cleaning a lot."

"He moved in the day before the car show. He never ate breakfast. He must have left early and stayed out all day. Oh, I remember one thing. He was Mr. No Cats! And I heard him talk to Dude one day up in the hallway."

"Oh, Mr. No Cats! Sneezy? He talked to Dude?"

"Yes, they talked for a long time. But they were way upstairs and I couldn't hear what they said." Aunt Dodo shut down the computer and started to cry. "All Dad's pow wow things are gone. I'm calling the police and EMT's for you. They need to look at your bump."

My head hurt and all I wanted to do was go to bed, but I knew I had to find the answers to a whole bunch of questions soon.

"Mrow?"

"Come here, boy. I need a hug before I see any EMT's again." I sat down on the sofa and leaned back onto a pillow. Huron padded over and lay on my chest.

He had another piece of pork rind and he chewed away at it with a little gurgling growl.

Fiero, Fiero. I couldn't understand why that name sounded so familiar? My stomach growled. I must still be growing... somewhere...mmm, I still had some fudge left. No, tacos would be better. Then the sign from the trailer on the corner of Little Bear's lot, FIERO'S FIERY CHILI AND TACOS, appeared in my brain. Mr. Sneezy must have brought the trailer to the car show. But why was the trailer sitting over there and why wasn't it open? I planned to check it out in the morning...after I scrubbed a million bathrooms.

CHAPTER THIRTY-FIVE

HOT STUFF

"Hey, Aunt Dodo, when did someone move into the old souvenir shop down the street?" Eric asked as he was leaving for work the next day.

"Didn't know they had. Mrs. Davis is in the nursing home so no one is living there that I know of."

"Hmm. I thought I saw a light in the window when I came home late last night, but maybe it was a reflection."

What old store? I got out of my chair and looked out the window as far as I could see to the left. A big red FOR SALE sign almost hid the little bark-covered building. I could tell whoever owned it probably sold Native American souvenirs a long time ago. A little teepee that matched the building sat in what used to be the parking lot. It looked like it might have been a place for kids to play. Now the yard was so brushy that the patched building almost disappeared into the woods behind it.

"Hey Eric, don't leave yet." I hustled into the hallway.

"Yo, Fudge Face, make it snappy. I gotta get the noon ferry."

"Let's check that place out when you get home tonight. I have a strange feeling about it."

"Now you boys be careful," Aunt Dodo said. "The 'for sale' sign went up this week and the real estate people are probably watching the property. If you cause a problem while looking around you might end up in jail. Besides, the building is probably stuffed full of old junk and is a fire hazard, too."

Hmm. What kind of old junk would be in a place like that?

"Are you sure Mrs. Davis is still in the nursing home?" I asked.

"Yes, Mrs. Davis is in her 90's and very healthy. She just can't walk. Our quilting group took her a lap quilt last Sunday. Why?"

"I was curious. When my great-grandma was in a nursing home, we couldn't sell her house."

"Oh, that's right. I'm going to call the home right now and see if she's okay." Aunt Dodo sat down at the desk and picked up the phone.

I jerked my thumb toward the door and whispered, "Are we on to look around tonight?"

"Yowser! See you after nine." And Eric ran for the ferry.

I went out on the porch and looked around the area again. Everything had changed during the night. The carnival trailer was now on the far side of the arena's parking lot, about twenty feet from the old shop.

Someone had changed the trailer's tires and taken down the food advertising signs. There were "Swap Meet Here" signs by the road and the arena lot was filling up fast. Soon the white trailer would disappear into the commotion until the show was over.

I didn't want to wait for Eric, but I knew I had to. I'll never go into something alone anymore. It was too dangerous. I decided to look at the cars that were in the lot and see if something else would turn up.

The whole parking lot looked like a carnival. Between each show car were tables of junk for sale. I saw food, car parts and car cleaning products, clothes, blankets, flags, leatherwork, and small fireworks. It was like a car flea market.

I had a fun and nasty idea. I went over to the fireworks man and looked over his display. Under the green striped canopy, he had boxes of Bang Snaps, sparklers and small bottle rockets. Then I saw a box of real stuff under a chair.

"What's that?" I asked the scruffy looking man.

"Oh, you're too young for that stuff. It's illegal." He pushed back his wide straw hat and grinned like a sly fox with slimy yellowish teeth.

"Too young for what?" I played dumber than usual.

"Blowing off your hand or face."

"Ha. You think I'm a dumb kid or something? Anyone can blow off a hand or face. I'll take five boxes of Bang Snaps, two strings of fire crackers, and a cherry bomb."

160

He picked up the cherry bomb up, but kept it tightly in his hand. "Cherry bombs are pretty noisy and dangerous."

"Yeah, so is my sister. She'll never forget what I have planned for her. Hand it over."

"Twenty bucks."

"What? That's way too much for this small amount of stuff." I couldn't believe the guy could charge so much for so little.

"You see anybody else selling this stuff around here?" He spit onto the ground and wiped his mouth with the hand that held the cherry bomb.

Ugh, gross! I'm not touching that man's hand.

I dug some of my fudge money out of my pocket and slapped it on the table. "All right, but I think you're robbing me."

I felt like a mad bomber when I shoved it all into my pants pockets. I wondered if I tripped and fell down, would my pants explode.

"Here." He threw something at me. "Heh heh heh," His laugh was annoying. "I'll toss in this lighter to help you destroy your life. Now don't tell anyone where you got that cherry bomb. My buddies and I make them, and they aren't legal in the US."

I decided to make him squirm a little for ripping me off. "Yea, I know. My dad's a state policeman..." I, too, can grin like a sly fox. The man's face turned as white as a snowdrift. "...but he's not here today, and this stuff will be long gone before he shows up. Heh, heh, heh." I strolled away and bought a bag of popcorn.

When I looked back, all the fireworks from the table were gone.

"Hmm, I wonder what else he and his buddies make and sell from under that chair?"

I took a walk around the lot and checked out the old carnival trailer from all sides. There were so many people wandering around the area that I blended in. Then I noticed the sticker on the back of the trailer. WILLIAMSTON MOTORS. I was so shocked I almost choked on my popcorn.

CHAPTER THIRTY-SIX

SACK? SACK? WHO HAS THE SACK?

All good detectives go on a stakeout occasionally. Observation is very important. Since Eric wouldn't be back until late, I figured I'd stick around and watch the people and the car show — and the trailer. I dragged a chair from the Inn's porch and parked myself under a tree like a compact car. I had a scenic view of everything — the Inn, arena parking lot, trailer, and the La Croix's home.

I had too many strings tangled up in my brain. I couldn't figure out why the trailer had a Williamston Motors sticker on the back. That business was right down the road from my home. Old Miss Ruffle/ Mr. Mustache or whoever it was in those ridiculous costumes had to be connected to the trailer somehow. Was Miss Ruffle/Mr. Mustache also Mr. No Cats? Who was the Wendigo? Who took Grandpa Redhawk's pow wow things? Why were they so interested in the old shop? The only thing I was sure of was that I wasn't sure of anything.

Car people like to talk about their cars so I yakked with a lot of people while I watched the area. It was the right time to hide in a crowd. I saw men in cowboy hats and boots, Hawaiian shirts and shorts, blonde haired women in bright flowered dresses, and people of every hue and shade in every kind of tee shirt ever made.

Dude left the tent and went toward downtown. Then I saw Teya leave the tent, and go into the La Croix's house carrying a sack. A few minutes later Dude casually strolled in from the street and went into the house carrying a stack of pizzas and a large white bag. A few minutes later Mr. Mustache came out of the house carrying what looked like the same sack. He looked suspiciously at the crowd, walked to the trailer through the swarm of people, opened the door and went in.

He was in there a long time, came out empty handed and walked back into the La Croix's house.

Next, Teya poked her head out the door, looked around and marched off to the trailer with a box. She stayed inside for a while and went back to the tents.

I felt as if I was watching a game of 'Sack, sack, who's got the sack.'

As the day went on the smell from the swap meet turned from car exhaust to grilling burgers. When no one from the La Croix's house carried anything else to the trailer, I figured they were done for the day. My stomach growled, so I headed home to eat dinner. As soon as Eric got home, the relaxing time would be over and the real detective work would begin.

I was in such a hurry to get back to my observation post, I plowed through my dinner. Aunt Dodo who was taking her turn cooking, limped over, put her hand on my head and said, "Are you feeling all right, Jared?"

"Yes, I'm okay. I need to get back outside and watch... the car show."

"I didn't know you liked cars." She looked puzzled and said, "Did you look at the blue one in the garage that belongs to Eric's dad?"

"No, not yet. Eric said he'd show it to me when he has a day off, so he'll probably show it to me tomorrow."

"I swear that kid never rests. He always works so hard." Aunt Dodo filled my glass with more milk and gave me a huge piece of cherry pie.

"Thanks, Aunt Dodo." My stomach was already close to bursting. "It's expensive to live on the island, so I guess he has to do what he can. Well," I pushed back from the table and stood up, "I better get going before I eat so much of your good food that I can't walk."

Becky and Sadie stomped in the back door as I was leaving. "Sorry we're late. What's cooking, Aunt Dodo? Smells good."

"Fried chicken, mashed potatoes and gravy. Sadie, you had better check on your brother. He's heading for the front door now. He only had one helping. I think he's sick."

I waddled out the door and headed for my observation chair. I was only gone about ten minutes. I didn't think anything could happen in that short time.

"Are you sick, Jared?" Sadie actually looked worried when she and Becky found me.

"Nah. I'm watching my suspects."

"That's good. I didn't think you were sick, but Aunt Dodo said you only had one helping of chicken."

"Sadie, she gave me four pieces for my first helping. Her chicken is delicious, but I'm so full I can't even burp. I could us your help watching the La Croix's house and the trailer. They've been carrying stuff from the tents and the house and putting it in the trailer most of the afternoon."

"Really?" Becky said. "I wonder what they are up to now."

"Do we have to?" Sadie moaned. "I hate watching people."

"Yes. If something bad happens I'll need you to run for help."

"All right. Remember, I do have my trusty phone and can call 911." She flipped it open and yelped, "Darn! My battery is dead! Sorry, Jared, I have to run back and plug it in for a while. With all the craziness going on last night, I must have forgotten to charge it."

About fifteen minutes later, the sack and box show started again. This time Teya and Dude took a tent down and carried it and a whole lot of suitcases and boxes to the trailer.

"Hmm. Are they leaving with the trailer?" I leaned forward to get up. Suddenly heavy hands slammed down on my shoulders and held me in my chair.

Chapter Thirty-seven

166

TRAPPED

"Hey, Fudge Breath, Dad let me off early. I had to eat a pile of chicken because Aunt Dodo said you ran out of the house as if you didn't like her food. Burp!"

"Didn't like her food? My plate had more food on it than my mom makes for our whole family! I ate four huge pieces of chicken."

"You slacker!" Eric tried to burp again. "I had six, but they were small. What's up?"

I showed Eric the cherry bomb. "You got any ideas for this and our sisters?"

"Whoa. What do you want to do, make them paraplegics?"

"Nah, only scare them a little."

"That will do it." Eric put his two index fingers into a cross shape. "Illeeee-gal. Where did you get it?"

I pointed. "From those guys over there with the box on the table. Do you want to visit them and see how fast they bury the box? I already dropped the 'my dad is a state policeman' statement."

He got an evil little grin on his face. "Let's stroll past and see what happens."

"We're back!" Sadie yelled in my ear. "I charged my battery and it's good for a while."

"That was fast! I'd hate to have you run down. I'd have to go look for your windup key."

Smack. "You're not funny, Jared."

"Ouch. Change of plans. I have an idea." I rubbed my head. "Let's go poke around the trailer and old shop and see what turns up."

"Boring," Becky said. "Isn't there anything else we can do?"

"Nope. That trailer is very busy right now and we have to find out why. But before you go, take these." I handed out the Bang Snaps. "Maybe they'll come in handy for something."

Sadie giggled and said, "Bang Snaps? What a bunch of wimpy fireworks. What can we do with these?"

"I don't know. Throw them or something. Now let's go!"

We went down the rows and looked for cool stuff but didn't find any. We walked past the fireworks man. He gave us a dirty look and shoved the box of illegal stuff into his car. "Get away, kid, you're bothering me," he said, then he spit.

"Yuck, he's gross." Sadie said with a curled lip. "I wonder if he ever spits on himself by accident."

The man turned to talk to somebody and scratched his armpit like a monkey with fleas. "Look at him. I'll bet he smells like a monkey, too," Becky sneered as she pitched a couple of Bang Snaps in his direction. She shoved the rest in her pocket when the guy jumped from the noise. "Cool idea, Jared. These things are great."

We noticed that some cars were lining up in the front driveway to start the big parade over the Mackinac Bridge, so we strolled over near the trailer and shop.

"Let's go try the back windows. Maybe we can see in and nobody will notice us." I thought I might set off the cherry bomb and scare the girls when they were tossing their Bang Snaps and looking at something else.

"Hey you guys," I hissed, "get down. That window is open." I grabbed Sadie's arm and pulled her aside. "I hear voices in there."

"Nobody's supposed to be in there," Eric said. "Aunt Dodo said Mrs. Davis is still living. She doesn't know where the sign came from because it's not for sale."

The whole building looked as if it was about to fall down. There were big gaps between the layers of bark siding where the cement chinking had fallen out. We could hear every word spoken inside. I crawled to the window and peeked in a crack between the water-stained curtain and the frame.

Teya was inside with her back to me. "Teya is in there!"

I heard Dude yell, "You may be my real father but I'm not doing anything you say. I don't care what Teya did. I'm not going to jail for taking stuff from graves!"

Seems like I've been here before. The last time it almost ended very badly.

Then I heard a smooth voice. "Bon, Thomas. Your sister will go to jail...and you will go back to France with me."

"No, I am his guardian. You can't do that," Teya said.

"My dear *fille*, you will have a bad name soon and won't be able to ahh, care for him..."

"Shaddap! Don't tell them what to do. Ha-choo! Gack, this place reeks of mold!" That voice was familiar but I didn't know why. "Shaddap everybody, I got to think...gotta get those other kids in here. They owe me big time."

Sadie started shaking and mumbling something.

I motioned Eric and Becky away from the building and dragged Sadie to the other side of the trailer.

I was shocked when Sadie grabbed me and started crying. Her face was so pale it gleamed in the sunset. "That voice is Ferel! He must have escaped from prison. That voice gave me nightmares for months. What are we going to do?"

"It is Ferel? Oh... now it all makes sense. He found us! He was Miss Ruffle next door, Mr. Mustache, and the man with the cowboy boots. He could have been anyone. He was always in costume."

Then it struck me. Ferel wasn't just pretending to be Miss Ruffle or Mr. Mustache, he was planning to kill us. Then I started to shake. *Be calm. Be calm.*

"Wait, Sadie. There's someone else in there. The Frenchman from the city clerk's office..."

"Oh no. Not two people? Wait...there are four bad guys in that house. Ferel, the Frenchman, Teya. And Dude, too? Is Dude good or bad?"

I hugged Sadie. "It's going to be okay. Think. If we call the police this could get wild. There are so many people in the parking lot all the bad guys could walk out of here and no one would see them. If they have a gun, they could cause a riot. Let's go find Eric and Becky and make some plans."

We went back to the window, and then worked our way around the store. Eric and Becky were nowhere in sight. All the doors seemed to be nailed shut. "How did everybody get inside?"

A high voice yelled, "You wait, you two evil monsters. When my Luke comes home, he will find you."

Then I heard Eric say, "Sit down, Aunt Lulu."

Ferel snorted, "Ha. Luke is useless… I fixed his wagon a long time ago."

"You big stinking rat face! I know you took my grandpa's stuff. Our whole tribe is going to curse you and I hope you die!" Becky yelled.

"Sit down, kid. I almost shot you once. I sure won't miss this time," Ferel growled.

"Be calm, little *fille*. We don't want to hurt you." The Frenchman's smooth voice almost convinced me.

"I don't trust you either, you sneaky slime bucket. You have your own kids tied up in here. And why did you hit my brother?"

"But I didn't want to…tie them up, they are just not in control. *Mon Dieu*…this is madness, Ferel. I just wanted a few bones from this place."

Sadie looked at me again with her mouth wide open. "He's got Eric and Becky and Aunt Lulu in there. How did he catch them? I'm going to call 911! Oh no, my phone is looking for service and the battery is almost dead again!"

My brain was in a whirl. I tapped my forehead until it stopped spinning. "Okay— think... think."

"How many people are in there?" Sadie asked.

I started counting aloud, "Teya, Dude, Becky, Eric, and Aunt Lulu; five and the Frenchman and Ferel, seven. If we find the door, we can open it and let people out. But since Ferel has a gun, we have to figure out a way to get him outside. Or everyone else out and keep him in." I don't think I made any sense to Sadie because I sure didn't make sense to me.

"Sadie, look! Here by the door." I whispered. "A bag of garbage with a pork rinds package in it. This must be the way in. Stay back." Sadie hid behind a tree and I bent down and tugged on the edge of the door. It moved enough to show that it was open. Like the dungeon door in the Haunted Hall on Mackinac Island, it only looked nailed shut.

"I have an idea." I leaned against the house and whispered to Sadie, "Go get the badminton net and we'll stretch it from the door to this tree and that tree over there. That way they can only go one direction when they open the door. Then we'll tie a rope knee-high to trip him. It will slow him down so we can grab his gun."

"Grab his gun?" Sadie's eyes got huge. "No way, Jared, he'll shoot us."

Then it hit me. I would waste my fireworks on him instead of Sadie.

"Let's go check the trailer and see what's so important." We went to the far side of the trailer again.

I kept watch while Sadie crept into the trailer. I heard a squeak of a scream, "Jared! It's packed with everything from the Inn and all kinds of old stuff —pictures, artwork, baskets, old jewelry and…and a big box of bones and dried up…medicine bags?"

"Hurry and get out of there."

Sadie crept out. "What do we do?"

"I'm going to check the Boney Collector. If the trailer hitch is big enough, I'm going to pull this trailer to the police station."

"But you didn't take driver's training yet."

"It's okay. I know enough. Now hide until I come back."

I ran to the tents and found Dude's keys on the picnic table. I drove as carefully as I could between the cars. I had a lot of practice hooking a car up to a trailer when I helped Aunt DJ, but there was no rear view mirror this time. And it was getting dark.

Some of the car people helped me as I backed up the Boney Collector and attached the trailer. No one suspected a thing.

"Sadie, please! Hide someplace. You can't come along with me. I'm going to throw some of these things into the store." I showed her the fireworks. "When I drive away they'll be really angry. I'm sure—I *know* the men will follow me. Then you go in and let everybody out. If he catches me… never mind, he's not going to… I gotta go. They're lining up for the parade and blocking the main street. I'm going down the back streets and find the police."

I ran up to the building, lit half the string of firecrackers and yelled, "Hey you slime buckets! Come and get me! I'm taking your trailer and all your goodies." I shoved the firecrackers into the window and ran to the car. Then I lit the other half of the string and pitched it onto the road. When it went off, I yelled, "Yahoo! Let's go!"

I pulled out of the parking lot and headed south on the road nearest the Inn. I watched the side view mirror and saw Ferel drag Becky along by her arm. She was kicking and screaming. Sadie jumped out from behind a tree and grabbed Becky's other arm. She yanked Becky free and they disappeared.

"Come on, you freaky old lady-man. Catch me if you can!" I yelled as I flew down the back road and headed for the police. At least I hoped to find the police—I didn't know where they were.

CHAPTER THIRTY-EIGHT

CATCH ME IF YOU CAN

I had never driven on a gravel road at night before. Heck, I had never driven on a gravel road at all. There weren't many around Williamston that our driver's training teacher had us drive on. This gravel caught the wheels on the trailer and made the car feel as if the trailer was going to flip over. Corners came up too fast. The box seat under me slid from side to side. The Boney Collector's brakes were lousy and it never stopped when I wanted it to. Cars from the show blocked every street I looked down.

"Police, police! Oh Lord! Where is the police station! Where are they when you need them?"

The road ended and I turned left. I turned and turned again. I prayed that Ferel had taken the bait and "borrowed someone's car" to chase me and let everyone escape. I kept an eye on my mirrors, but I never saw any headlights following me.

I finally turned again and found myself on an unmarked dead end road. I pounded the steering wheel and shouted, "Nooo! I've never backed up a trailer. How to I get out of here?"

I saw that the narrow road circled around a streetlight and doubled back. I hoped the trailer would be able to make the turn without getting stuck on something.

I was so careful. There were too many valuable things in the trailer to crash it and Dude's car was so important to him, I couldn't ruin it either. I had completed the circle without any scratches when I saw car lights down the street coming right at me. "Yikes! It's him!"

I hit the gas. If it was Ferel, I wasn't going to let him get a good shot at me. If it wasn't him, I still wasn't going to stop. "Go! Go! Go!" I yelled and stepped harder on the gas.

The bright blue car turned in front of me as if it was part of a police chase, but there weren't any red and blue lights flashing so I wasn't going to stop. I turned halfway into a driveway and drove across someone's front yard. I heard a crunch and a thump and the mailbox went flying.

"Sorry!" I apologized to the people whose mailbox I killed, "but I want to live to see another day." I could feel the tickets piling up. Under age, unlicensed driver driving too fast for conditions, stealing private property, destroying property, and then causing the death of a minor— my dad would do that one if Ferel didn't catch me first.

I heard a crack and the corner of my windshield burst into fragments. "It is him! Please car! Go! Go! Go!"

I careened to a stop at a busy highway that I figured was US-2. I knew the state police post was north of town on I-75, and the entrance to I-75 was someplace to the right of where I was and that's all I knew. I frantically looked back and forth. All of a sudden, I saw emergency lights flashing. Two police cars sat in a parking lot across the road looking right at me. I flashed my lights and they flashed back. They were the answer to the prayers I had screamed out as I drove.

I saw bright lights behind me coming up fast in my mirror, but there was a semi barreling down on me from the left. I held my breath and blew across the five lanes right in front of the truck. "Sorry, Mr. Truck Driver," I said. The driver hit his brakes and honked long and loud. He missed me by inches. I slid into the parking lot and blocked the police cars from Ferel's view.

I jumped out and ran to them as fast as I could get out of the car.

"Don't shoot me! I'm Jared Daly. The trailer is full of stolen goods. An escaped prisoner in that car across the highway is chasing me and he's got a gun."

I sat on the ground and put my hands behind my head.

"No problem, sir. We've been waiting for you," one officer said. "What took you so long?"

"Get back in the car, Mr. Daly," the other officer said. The other officer named Luke La Croix.

CHAPTER THIRTY-NINE

I'M THE BAIT? ME?

The bright blue car flew across the five-lane highway as fast as I did, but the driver didn't see anyone but me. Ferel jumped out of a sports car that sparkled like a blue diamond in the lights. I saw someone else in the passenger's seat. The Frenchman was along for the ride.

Ferel raised the gun at me, "Kid, get ready to die. You have been irritating me for too long."

I couldn't move, except for the violent shaking of my body. All I could do was think, *Hurry, hurry! He's going to shoot me!*

"Drop it, Ferel. You're under arrest," a voice said from the side.

"What? Is that La Croix?" I ducked, and Ferel's gun went off…twice.

Sorry about your car window, Dude. I thought as the whole front window exploded and a sharp pain slammed into my shoulder.

When I woke up, I was in an ambulance.

"You passed out," the medic said. "The bullet scratched you and you have a few tiny cuts from the flying glass, but you'll be fine."

I could barely talk my teeth were chattering so hard. "I could have thrown up instead of passing out. I don't like looking down the barrel of someone's gun. It freaks me out."

"Same here," the medic agreed, and poked me with a big needle.

Sadie and Mom showed up at the emergency room a couple of hours later. A friend of the Redhawk's had flown Mom off the island in their small airplane.

"Sorry. When I left with the trailer I didn't have a cell phone, and there wasn't time to call anyone," I apologized.

Sadie sniffed and wiped her eyes. "I finally got some bars on my phone after you left and called 911. Then my phone died again and I didn't know if they understood me."

Becky ran in the door and kissed me on the cheek. "The hero has landed. Great job saving the world, **Bay-bee-misay-si**! That means whirlwind. I saw you fly down that dirt road driving the Boney Collector."

I think my face turned as red as the emergency lights on an ambulance.

"Whoa, Becky, did you call him 'baby'?" Eric said. "Calm down, you two, or my aunts will start planning a big party."

CHAPTER FORTY

TYING SOME ENDS TOGETHER

The police knew Ferel had escaped, but they didn't think he was dangerous enough to tell us. I guess he thought dressing up like an ugly old woman, moving in next door and playing nasty pranks was a good way to start taking his revenge. Who in their right mind would want to look that bad? He hated us, so I guess that explains it all. He is going back to jail, hopefully a big strong, impenetrable prison fortress.

The Frenchman called himself Jacques Marquette. He had been in the same cell as Ferel. Together they hatched the idea of proving his claim to the Marquette family home in Laon, France. Weird. The cost of running DNA testing on every scrap of bone Teya dug up would have been extremely expensive. The whole idea was ridiculous.

The police looked in all the places Ferel had been and found his stash of costumes and makeup. He is so good with makeup, Sadie should take some lessons from him. He wasn't the Wendigo, the Frenchman was, but Ferel did his make-up. Ferel kidnapped Aunt Lulu to keep Teya and Dude in line and made everyone fill the trailer with all the things he wanted, along with the Frenchman's boxes of bones.

The Boney Collector survived the wild ride, but Dude got a ticket for not having the proper seating and seatbelts in the car. Ferel took Eric's father's car from their garage. That's why he caught me so quickly. That old Camaro is a speed demon.

All the stuff in the trailer survived and went back to the original owners except for the things that were in the old store. They went into the Partridge's basement to keep for Mrs. Davis. When I threw the fireworks into the store, they got stuck in the window frame, blew up and caught the old store on fire. Luckily, everybody got out before it went up in flames. I guess Mrs. Davis won't have to worry about the old building anymore.

Dude won't go to jail. Teya on the other hand might have to go to jail for a short time. It depends on her judge. The Frenchman really is their father. I feel sorry for them because he's a total lunatic.

The Frenchman forced Teya and Dude to do all the digging and stealing of artifacts from the graves. If only Teya had asked for some help at the museum instead of leaving the door open for Ferel. Because I had the pictures to show the police, it proved that he planned to take even more things from the museum.

Luke was finally home. He had been undercover and wasn't allowed to contact anyone. He knew nothing about Teya and her schemes.

And me. The EMT's found my cherry bomb and gave it to the police. I have to pay a fine for that, and on all those driving tickets I got. I may never get to take driver's education until I'm 50 years old.

Even though I saved Becky, Eric, Aunt Lulu, Teya, and Dude, crime does not pay *you—you* pay for it. "ARRGH!"